Towers
The Ellison Legacy Part One

Foundation

Carol A. McDuffy

TM

ENESKAY Publishing
Philadelphia, PA

Six Towers (Towers Series)
Copyright 2010 by Carol A. McDuffy. All rights reserved.

For Information Contact: **ENESKAY** Publishing, LLC
The Cedar Works
4919 Pentridge Street
Philadelphia, PA 19143-3318

Cover Photo: Dennis D. McDuffy

Website: camcduffy.com

Email: eneskay.us@gmail.com
carolamcduffy@gmail.com

Library of Congress Control Number: 2010942440
McDuffy, Carol A.
Six Towers (Towers 1 - Foundation)
ISBN 978-0-9844851-4-7

ABOUT THE AUTHOR

Carol A. McDuffy is an author of fiction and poetry and Principal of **ENESKAY Publishing**. Carol has a background in Human Behavior & Development, Information Technology & Process Management. Writing is her passion. She lives in Philadelphia, PA - U. S. A.

Novels: **"Unintentional"** (a fictional novella)

"Towers" (fictional series novels)
1. Foundation
2. Stronger than Steel
3. Built to Last

Short Story: **"Chocolate Child"** (science fiction)

Poetry: **"LIFE Poems"** (four volumes)
Volume 1: **Love**
Volume 2: **Inspiration**
Volume 3: **Forgiveness**
Volume 4: **Evolution**

This book was written to acknowledge the honorable men in my life. You taught, influenced, challenged, counseled and loved me. I am blessed and fortunate to be your granddaughter, daughter, sister, wife, lover, mother, grandmother, aunt, niece, cousin and friend.

Princes, Kings and Heroes,

I Love You All!

1st Generation
Fredrick Bishop
William E. Cheeks
Thomas Fant Sr.
John D. McDuffy
George Whitmore

2nd Generation
Eugene McDuffy
James W. Palmer

3rd Generation
Joseph Allston
Daniel Cooper
Ronald Cooper
Mark Davis
Joseph Fields
Robert Hagler
Othniel Hibbert
Byron James
Shawn P. Kimble
Dennis D. McDuffy
Eugene V. McDuffy II
Jerome McKinnon
James Nelson
Michael J. Owens
Brian Thomas
Jerome L. Whitehead

4th Generation
Shawn J. Kimble
Kyle J. Kimble
Tahseem Jeffries
Todd Jeffries
Jeffrey Jones
Eugene McDuffy III
Paul McDuffy
Floyd Payne
Taiman Richardson
Anthony Wheeler
Daniel Williams

5th Generation
Tyler A. Kimble

To

Flatty and Peewee

with Love

Towers

The Ellison Legacy Part One

Foundation

Carol A. McDuffy

Chapter One
ELLISONS – The New Land

Migration

Charles Randolph was the last surviving son of Randolph and Beulah-Mae Ellison. Born in the United States of America, he lived in Georgia outside the town of Savannah. He lived on the land his family owned since the emancipation of slaves. His people were buried on it including his brother.

The Ellison farmland was surrounded by natural woodlands, beautiful flowering gardens and age-old trees covered with Spanish moss. CharlesR experienced reoccurring vivid nightmares about the trees. The trees turned into giant root-walking monsters. The Spanish moss clinging to the gnarled branches transformed into white men with glowing white eyes; dressed in long white robes and white hoods. The white men carried thick ropes, each with a noose at the end and Jim Crow was leading them all straight to the Ellison farm.

In the early nineteen hundreds, 'Jim Crow laws' were used in the southern states to enforce racial segregation between whites and non-whites. 'Jim Crow' meant a litany of rules resulting in poor educational facilities and limited job opportunities for the 'Colored.' Breaking Jim Crow laws came with severe punishment.

The Colored, 'Blacks,' were terrorized by cross-burnings where they lived and the frequent lynching of black men, women and children were unchecked by southern law. The 'good ole south' was not a safe place for CharlesR.

Ninety percent of the African-American population lived in the Southern states but oppression and violence targeted toward southern Blacks forced many Black people to uproot their families to survive. North-east cities were prime destinations. There were no Jim Crow laws in the North. The Great Migration of African Americans out of the rural south to the urban cities in the Northeast, Mid-west and West between 1916 and 1970 was one of the largest and most rapid mass movements in American history.

Randolph Ellison was responsible for the Ellison farmland but his son, CharlesR was not obligated to stay. Randolph needed to protect CharlesR. He wanted CharlesR to have a chance for a longer life than his first born son. He knew some folks who moved from Savanah and settled in Philadelphia, Pennsylvania. Philadelphia was an evolved northeastern city with an economic and educational hub of universities and colleges. Randolph used the 'Black-Folks Network' and arranged for CharlesR to relocate. CharlesR would live with a trusted family in Philadelphia. He would pay for his room and board by repairing the family's house until he found steady employment and a place of his own.

Farming was the primary source of income for the Ellison's but leaving the security of the farmland was a necessity for CharlesR. Migration from the South to the North opened up opportunities for him to seek a better education, a better job and income or start a business. Migration from the South was a way for CharlesR to secure a better future.

CharlesR stood in the early morning sun ready to board the back of an outbound train to Philadelphia. He was dressed in his church suit, a white shirt his mother hand scrubbed immaculately clean; and his father's navy blue bow tie. His Sunday shoes were polished with a spit-shine. His father handed him an old weathered suitcase with his belongings and a wrapped parcel containing winter socks and boots. CharlesR purchased the socks and boots himself with the money he earned building and mending fences for the neighboring farmers.

Randolph pulled a few dollars out the front pocket of his overalls, it was his share of the fence money he saved to give to CharlesR. He pressed the folded bills into CharlesR's hand then he pulled out something else from his pocket wrapped in wax-paper. Randolph tucked it inside the hidden pocket of CharlesR's suit jacket. "The money ain't much, but it'll help ya some. The seeds is more valuable. You make em grow and you ain't never gon' be hungry. I know ya gonna make us proud Son." Randolph gave his son a hug and pat on the back to express everything he did not say.

Beulah smiled but her eyes expressed her true feelings. She was sad, fighting back her tears as she handed CharlesR a large whicker basket.

"I packed you some fried chicken, cornbread and ders a jar of sweet tea I wrapped in a tablecloth but be careful so it don't break. I fiddin' dat'ill keep you over the long train ride, and dere's plenty of fruit, boiled peanuts and dose figs you like. I even slipped in a sweet potato pie before your Daddy got to it. You can share it out when you git dere."

Beulah touched her son's chin gently. She traced the dimple he inherited from her father. CharlesR kissed his mother's hand then hugged her tight so she could feel his appreciation for her loving care. She held him close and the soft southern drawl of her voice was a soothing balm in his ear. "You make sho ta write and tell us how things is when you get to the city. Dere's postage stamps in the basket too."

He replied obediently, "Yes Ma'am."

She whispered, "I love you son."

Their embrace did not last long enough for CharlesR. He was already homesick for his father; his mother; his family; his favorite foods and his home on the farm. The realization of leaving behind all that was familiar made him feel like he was all alone in the world; before he loss the battle with his own tears he turned and stepped up onto the train car.

CharlesR was on his way to new land seven hundred miles away from the only home he knew. He had no idea what he would find but he intended to make his father and mother proud by building a new foundation for the Ellison family in the North. He waved goodbye as the train pulled away not knowing when or if he would ever see his father and mother again. Charles Randolph Ellison was seventeen. It was 1948.

Raising Towers

Eight years before CharlesR pulled out of the Savanah train station, CoraLee Alexander's family moved to Philadelphia. The Alexanders took advantage of the industrial jobs created by the expansion of the Pennsylvania Railroad. It was also the Alexander family's escape from the South and the disrespect and humiliation they suffered fighting and loosing the rightful claim to their land through a rigged court system.

CoraLee was a devout Christian, intelligent, resourceful and beautiful. She was in charge of directing the repairs in the church building her family regularly attended. When CharlesR was hired as the new handyman CoraLee liked him right away; he was young but she thought he was mature for his age. He was a great communicator and he followed directions well. His southern charm was refreshing and he treated CoraLee with respect.

CharlesR finished all the repairs for the contracted fee in record time, then volunteered his free time and construction skills to CoraLee's church. He started attending church regularly, he enjoyed spending time with CoraLee and the Alexanders. Soon he put together a small group of men from the church to assist him with building wooden flower-boxes to brighten up the outside entrance. By the end of the year CharlesR added a vegetable garden and a decorative gazebo with seating. CoraLee took before and after pictures and had them developed for CharlesR to show people. When people saw the improvements CharlesR was hired by members of the church and neighboring community to make improvements on their homes.

CharlesR wrote a letter to CoraLee expressing his affection and romantic feelings. He also admitted he wrote about her to his parents. CharlesR and CoraLee's friendship turned into a very brief courtship because they saw no point in delaying their desire to become husband and wife.

The Alexander-Ellison wedding was a chance for the families to have a long-awaited reunion. Randolph and Beulah were getting up in age but they made the train ride to Philadelphia and celebrated with youthful exuberance. They were proud their son was prospering and adding another branch to the Ellison family tree.

The Ellisons and Alexanders put their money together to help the newlyweds put a downpayment on a house. CharlesR found a three-story victorian with six bedrooms. It was a fixer-upper in need of repair, but CharlesR knew he could make it a comfortable home.

Charles Randolph and CoraLee Ellison moved into their home and started a family right away. CharlesR was twenty and Cora-Lee was twenty-four when their first child was born and the babies kept coming.

The first born, Charles Randolph Ellison Jr. inherited his father's cleft chin.

Paul Mansa was born eleven months after Charles Jr.. He was a duplicate copy of his older brother minus the dimpled chin.

Joseph Martin was born a year after Paul. Ronald James and Byron Alexander followed in succession each two years apart.

CoraLee had difficulty giving birth to Eugene Vincent; he came early. He was the smallest premature baby in the hospital but he was strong. They called him 'Peewee.' Peewee was the last child CoraLee would be able to carry, but with six children CoraLee and CharlesR felt abundantly blessed.

Family

Family was important to CharlesR and CoraLee. Family was the foundation of their future. They raised their boys with unconditional love, unwavering faith and an appreciation for each child's individuality.

CoraLee rose early in the mornings, first to pray, then to run her busy household. She prepared delicious healthy meals for her family from her husband's organic garden. She made sure her children stayed focused on their education. She insisted they never miss a day of school and to be home in time for dinner. She tutored them during their frequent visits to the free library. Sundays, with CharlesR, she led her boys to Sunday school and church service. CoraLee shared her belief with her children that even though they would eventually grow bigger and stronger they would never match the power of the Almighty God. She stressed the importance of faith. She told them faith would be their ultimate strength and it would be tested many times. She advised them to put their trust in a higher power and it would lead them to their destiny. She encouraged each of her sons to follow their own path using their unique God-given talents.

CharlesR and CoraLee taught the boys about their African and American heritage. CoraLee was a Black Queen and she ruled along side her Black King. She called her sons Princes. She taught the Princes their ancestors did not come to America by choice. She taught them about the history of Europeans and Euro-Colonists kidnapping and stealing Africans from their homeland to enslave them. She told them, "Never forget you come from African Kings, Queens, Chieftains, Agriculturalists, Environmentalists, Architects, Astronomers, Engineers, Scientist and Healers. You are to remain humble but walk with your heads held high to reflect the dignity and pride of your ancestors."

CoraLee was given a collection of the Ellison family historical documents and records from her mother-in-law, Beulah Mae Harper-Ellison. The collection included pictures of Ellison land before and after the civil war showing the slow but steady expansion of the farm. Wrapped in a lace handkerchief was a wedding photo of Randolph and Beulah along with a photo of Beulah with her two sons, Randolph Junior and CharlesR. There were no other pictures of Randolph Junior. There were a few pictures of CharlesR growing up on the farm and one of his father Randolph sitting on a tractor. Beulah surprised CharlesR and CoraLee with a small portrait of her father, George Harper. She kept it in a velvet-lined wooden box. It was the only existing portrait of George. It was a very old painted photograph but it was in mint condition. The fissure deep inside George Harper's chin was clearly visible and CharlesR's resemblance to his grandfather was undeniable. Beulah said her father was a good man she wished her sons had a chance to get to know. There was a death certificate for George Harper but no cause of death was listed; the same omission was on Randolph Junior's death certificate. CoraLee did not pry about the circumstances but she had empathy for the Ellisons. She stored the documents and priceless treasures in a heavy cedar-wood chest her father-in-law Randolph made.

CoraLee became the entrusted Ellison and Alexander family historian and record keeper. She kept archives of birth and death records and shared the vast collection of photographs from albums and scrapbooks with her children. She had pictures of relatives and articles about the famous an infamous people in the family. The scrapbooks were full of original newspaper clippings. She told her children the factual stories behind the pictures, including the good, the bad and the ugly. Her hands always trembled when she turned to the page with a graphic picture of a lynching. The photo was faded and frayed but it was clear enough to recognize the naked and charred body hanging from the tree was a young Black boy. CharlesR would sit close to Cora-Lee and put his arm around her shoulder while she retold the terrible crime she witnessed.

CharlesR told his sons to remember Black men and women gave their lives for freedom and equality but there was still a struggle for Black people in America. He said they were never to complain because others had suffered worse atrocities. CharlesR remembered the cruelty of the South he escaped and he shared his experiences. He never spoke about his older brother but he gave his sons tools to survive and thrive in a country that was not welcoming to Black boys and Black men. CharlesR told his sons no man was perfect but every man must accept responsibility for his actions. He told them to strive for success in whatever they chose to pursue. He told them they had an obligation to get a good education and fulfill their roles as leaders for Black men in their community. CharlesR led by an example he expected his sons to follow.

He helped his six sons understand the key to their

survival in America. In one of his frequent lectures he gave them his edict. "African families were separated and enslaved by Europeans and Colonist. They were denied their own language, history and culture. That's why it's important for us Ellisons to maintain records of our own history and preserve our culture. We are not enslaved anymore. We are not bonded to white masters. We are bonded by our family blood. We are our own masters. The past has shown us when we are divided we are weak but when united we are strong. The Ellison bloodline is strengthened because of all of you. We must always stay united."

CharlesR was trying to keep his promise of making his mother and father proud and building the family. Every summer vacation he piled his wife and children into the station wagon and drove down south to visit and pay respect to their elders. Pop-Pop Rand and Nana Beulah were amazed at how much their grandsons grew between each visit. Randolph was impressed by their schoolbook smarts and knowledge about the family history. It astonished him that his only son fathered six sons to carry-on the Ellison name. Randolph thought CharlesR and CoraLee were doing a good job raising their boys. Beulah declared all the boys ate a hundred times their weight just like CharlesR did when he was a growing boy. She cooked and baked everyone's favorites during their summer visits. She was pleased CharlesR found a faithful wife and a loving mother for his children. Beulah enjoyed sharing Ellison family history with CoraLee. Every summer Beulah gave CoraLee more stories and pictures she collected between visits. CoraLee added them to the family archives.

African DNA was dominant in the Ellison family. Skin dark and rich with melanin over lean muscle and strong bone were common family traits. The Ellison Boys were taller than their mother by middle school and taller than their father by high-school. Charles Jr. and Paul grew to be the tallest, six-feet-seven inches. Joseph, Ronald and Byron were evenly matched at six-six. Peewee was still the smallest of the six siblings, yet at six-feet-four-inches he was a giant compared to boys his age. They were all growing into fine young men, healthy in mind, body and spirit. There were arguments between them and a bruise or two, but fights ended with a handshake and the brothers reunited.

Towers Part 1 - Foundation

Chapter Two
PAUL - Coming of Age

Rubin

Rubin tried to outrun them but he was surrounded. The taunts that started in school continued in the street. This time with no adults nearby the bullies were bolder and the ugly slurs were full of profanity.

Someone from the group shouted, "Fuckin' white trash! Little faggot!" A skinny, buck-toothed boy, eager to get in on the action questioned Rubin. "Are you a faggot white boy? I wonder if you even gotta a dick. You gotta a pussy little faggot?"

The boy who was the leader of the group touched Rubin's hair. He shouted to his gang, "Look at his hair, it's long like a fuckin' white girl!" All the other boys laughed and agreed Rubin's hair was long like a white girl. One boy with a serious bad case of acne asked, "Who ya daddy?... cause we know you ain't got your Momma's hair."

The skinny, buck-toothed boy shouted, "YA MOMMA BIG, BLACK AND FAT! YA MOMMA LOOK LIKE A BUTT CRACK!" The boys thought Skinny-Boy was hilarious. They laughed hysterically because they saw Rubin's mother at the school, she was a big-boned, dark skinned woman with a short afro.

Rubin tried to shut out their voices, he refused to let them see how much their words hurt. He thought if he did not react they would get bored and eventually leave him alone. He did not know the boys were just waiting for the leader to give the orders for the next move.

The leader stood back while the other four boys closed in and trapped Rubin in the middle of a tight circle. Close enough for their spit to fly in his face, they started a new barrage of cruel and vicious name calling. Rubin tried to step out of the circle, Skinny-Boy blocked his escape and shoved him then yelled, "Little pussy with hippy hair. I bet somebody sticking it up his ass and he likes it."

Rubin heard a sympathetic plea. It came from the leader. "Yo that's enough, he ain't worth it. Let's get outta here."

The other boys opened up the circle to let Rubin pass. Rubin was relieved the beatdown was over before it started. The leader acted as if he intended to let Rubin go, then he reached out and grabbed a fist full of Rubin's hair. This time he pulled it. He yanked it so hard there was a ripping sound.

Rubin screamed and dropped to his knees when his hair was torn out of his scalp by the roots. It felt like a blowtorch was put to his scalp. Uncontrollable tears filled his eyes as he touched the spot on his head that was on fire. His fingers felt something wet and mushy where hair should have been and Rubin stared in disbelief at the blood on his fingertips.

The leader laughed after he tossed Rubin's hair in the street. Proud of his accomplishment he shouted, "Fucking Halfbreed Faggot!"

Charles Jr., Paul, Joey and Ronnie were on their way to play stick ball on a dirt lot not far from the school; when they turned around the corner and saw Rubin on his knees with five boys circling him.

Paul said, "That's Rubin, the new boy in my class." Ronnie frowned, "Looks like Rubin is about to get his ass kicked by Jimmy and his boys."

Paul was holding the mop handle they used for a bat. Ronnie and Joey had the half-balls. They were all ready to toss everything aside and jump into action if their eldest brother gave the word.

Rubin attacked. He zeroed-in on the boy that pulled his hair out. He aimed his foot with his white high-top Chuck Taylor All Stars at the boy's kneecap. He kicked it with all his might. Jimmy stopped laughing, he cried out in pain and fell to the pavement holding onto his injured knee. Jimmy's gang looked helpless, then they ran towards Rubin. The Ellisons ran to the brawl but not before Rubin collided with Jimmy's boys. Rubin had fighting skills. His fist delivered punches, his feet kicked and every strike connected to his tormentors. He was quick. Jimmy and his gang never had a chance.

Paul, the fastest of the Ellison brothers, reached Rubin first but it took all four brothers to pull Rubin off of the other boys. Paul took Rubin aside to calm him down while Joey checked his bleeding head. Ronnie and Charles attended to the wounded gang on the ground. The injuries to Jimmy and his four boys included black eyes, bloody noses, bruised ribs and one dislocated patellar. Everyone heard Jimmy scream like a little girl when Joey snapped Jimmy's kneecap back into place. The knee was swelling, but Joey could tell it was okay. Jimmy was grateful there was less pain and he was able to walk. He was especially thankful to Joey that he would not need to explain to his no-nonsense mother why he had to go to the hospital.

After that fight, Jimmy and his gang never picked on Rubin again. They avoided Rubin when they saw him in school. Rubin loss a little hair that day but he won a lot of respect. The fight was the start of Rubin's life-long friendship with Paul.

ReeRee

The Civil Rights movement started with grassroots organizing, non-violent protest and boycotts in the 1950s' achieved a historic legislative gain for African Americans in 1964. President Johnson signed the Civil Rights Act into law, it outlawed discrimination in public accommodations including privately owned restaurants, hotels, stores, workplaces and schools.

Paul Ellison was experiencing his teenage years three years after the Civil Rights Act was signed. He attended a racially integrated all boys high-school. His grandfather, Randolph would have fully appreciated how times had changed but for Paul, it was just a normal high school year and time for the annual school play. The boys played all the roles; it was a school tradition and a forced choice in an all boys school. Paul had no interest in playing any role, Paul was happy with building the stage sets. Mr. Tate, the shop teacher, said Paul was the best builder in his class and his detail work improved every year. Paul enjoyed working behind the scenes creating realistic sets for the plays. His skills and talent shined bright under the stage lights. His stage sets always received compliments from the audience.

On the evening of the play Paul peeped out into the

audience from behind the curtains. Rubin's sister, Rita, was seated in the front row. She came to see the play with her classmates from the all girls high school. Paul thought Rita was the prettiest girl in the audience. He caught up with her after the play ended.

Rita told Paul she came because Rubin said Paul was in the play. She said the play was good but she was disappointed because she expected Paul to be acting in the play. She said she wanted to be an actor. Paul pointed to the mimeographed program Rita held in her hand. *Set Designs created by Mansa Ellison'* was printed under the credits. Paul explained he used his middle name. Rita said the set designs were spectacular. Paul thanked her for the compliment. Rita asked if she could have one of the set pieces.

"I want the one of the archway from the medieval scene. I can pay for it. Can you bring it to my house? We live up in the Lane now." Rita smiled proudly.

"Yeah, Rubin told me ya'll moved after the funeral. I'm really sorry about your Mom." Paul looked concerned when he asked, "How's Rubin doing? I haven't seen him in school." Rita's smile turned into a scowl. "Are you coming to see me or my brother?" Paul asked her, "What's your new address?" Rita wrote it down on a torn piece of paper and handed it to him while her girlfriends pretended not to notice, then with a wave at Paul she hurried off to join her friends. Paul grinned from ear to ear when he read the note. Rita drew a heart after the address and signed it, "*ReeRee.*"

A week later Paul wrapped the heavy set piece, carried it down the steps of the subway and stood over it on the long subway train ride to the Lane. He hoisted it up the subway steps carefully, then walked two blocks to Rubin and Rita's new house. Paul did it all for ReeRee. Rubin was not home.

Paul refused to accept ReeRee's money so she gave him two packs of subway tokens. After the exchange, Paul started taking the subway with ReeRee up to the Lane on Fridays after school. The Lane was far away from his neighborhood and brothers. Paul considered it a bonus. He spent time with ReeRee at her house talking and playing the records he borrowed from Peewee's collection. They listened to love songs while kissing. ReeRee was a good french-kisser.

Paul was not a virgin courtesy of a girl who asked him to escort her to her senior prom. He was only a sophomore but he fulfilled her desire before she went off to college. Paul suspected ReeRee was not a virgin either, but she would never let him go too far and so he respected her boundaries. ReeRee made him feel happy.

Going Steady

Rubin gave Paul a 'sliding-low-five' with one hand as he lifted up the garage door in the back of the house. Paul still needed to duck under to get inside.

"What's happenin Rubin?"

"Hey Paulie! My Man! Ain't nothing shakin but the bacon! ReeRee ain't here, she shopping ...she still spending her part of the insurance money."

The small garage was filled with the strong scent of marijuana. Paul ignored the smell and grabbed the empty milk crates he found in a corner. He stacked them on top of each other and used them to sit and stretch out his long legs. Rubin sank back into a new metal and woven vinyl lounge chair. He adjusted the chair to the upright position while he checked Paul out. He said, "Shiiiit, Paulie all y'all Ellisons is big."

Paul was used to questions, comments, and consequences related to his height. He shifted his butt on the uncomfortable crates. Rubin pulled out an expertly rolled joint from under his cap. Strands of his long hair escaped, there was no evidence he ever loss any from the fight the year before. He adjusted his cap and stuffed his hair back under it.

"So you and my sis going steady now?" Rubin asked laughing. "Shiiiit I know you ain't been coming all the way up here on a regular to see me." Paul admitted nothing. Rubin reached out and offered his hand palm up. Paul slapped it and Rubin slapped his in return. "It's cool man. You know you my bro. Shiiiit, she could do worse." Paul took Rubin's comment as his approval.

Rubin reached into the pocket of his grease stained work-overalls. He took out a book of matches with the faces of the three Pep Boys on the front cover. He lit the joint on the first strike of the matchstick and took a long drag, then offered the joint to Paul. "You wanna toke?... This some good shit."

"Nah man I don't smoke." Paul said and turned his face away to avoid getting a contact-high.

Rubin was not offended, he shrugged his shoulders and took another long drag. This time he let the smoke slip out of his mouth a little and inhaled it through both his nostrils to emphasize how good it was. Then he choked and had a coughing fit as the smoke forced itself out of his lungs. Rubin bragged while he coughed and gagged. "This some real bad-ass shiiiit. It il' get yo' head right. You sho you don't wanna a hit?"

"Nah, but I can see how bad it must be," Paul said.

Rubin was high so he missed Paul's sarcasm. He pounded on his chest as tears came to his red eyes then he took another drag. Paul watched as Rubin closed his eyes and held the smoke in longer. Paul decided it was time to make his getaway. He put the milk crates back where he found them and told Rubin, "Imma wait for Rita on the front porch, catch you later." Rubin nodded and repositioned the lounge chair so he could recline. Paul inhaled the fresh air as he walked around to the front porch to wait for his girlfriend to come home.

Wrong Side of the Tracks

A series of gun shots hit the wall behind Paul and the plaster was peppered with holes. Paul dropped to the floor. He felt a whoosh of air pass by then he heard a bullet shatter a window. He was close enough to the shooter to smell the smoke from the gun as more bullets ricocheted off the furniture. Projectiles flew through the air as Paul crawled on the floor looking for an escape. Rubin pushed him up and out through the broken window. Paul lost his balance and he snapped apart the window frame. He went crashing down onto the broken glass outside on the porch. He cut his arm but he did not have time to check the damage; he got up and started running for his life; he did not look back, he knew it might seal his doom. He saw Rubin running ahead of him until Rubin squeezed between the gap of a locked chain-linked fence and was out of sight. Paul set off in a sprint toward the fence. He was a fast runner but there was no way he would be able to fit through the narrow gate opening so he hurdled over the fence.

Paul caught up to Rubin and kept a sharp lookout until they were out of the Calumet Gang's territory. They walked in silence to the public transportation center and

Paul had time to think and process what happened. The cut on his arm was superficial. He was not angry with Rubin, he was angry with himself for believing Rubin's lies.

Rubin said he was going to a friend's late-night house-party. He said ReeRee would be there and he offered to pay Paul's subway fare if he came along. Paul was so preoccupied with the possibility of a slow-drag dance with ReeRee he did not think about the risk of going to a party in an unknown neighborhood.

The house was full of girls when they arrived. Paul had never seen any of them before and ReeRee was nowhere in sight. The girls were dancing to music on the stereo or chatting in little groups. None of the girls seemed to know Rubin. They looked at him with suspicion. A group of boys arrived and the trouble started. The boys were pissed-off Rubin and Paul showed up uninvited. Rubin and Paul had crashed the gangs's private after-hours party hosted by the gang leader's girlfriend. The Calumet Gang was notoriously armed. Paul was lucky he was catching the subway-train back home instead catching bullets in some gangster-girl's house. Paul still could not believe he was not dead on the floor.

After midnight the subway trains only ran every hour. It was past two in the morning, no one from the Lane rode the late trains. Paul and Rubin took the stairs down to the subway station entrance. No one was in the booth to collect the fare, Rubin ducked under the turnstile; Paul took a giant step over it. The subway-train was waiting at the station platform with the doors open. They boarded the middle car. They were the only two passengers. Rubin moved forward between each of the empty train-cars by sliding open the doors and hopping across the uneven gaps to the next car. His destination was the front car. Paul stepped over the gaps and ducked under the doorways to avoid hitting his head.

Rubin reached the front car, he tried to open the operator door, it was unlocked and unoccupied. The locomotive's engine was in stand-by mode while the train operator was on a break. Rubin took the engineer's seat, turned the key, closed all the train doors, released the brakes and started to drive the train down the track through the tunnel.

Paul was still making his way to the front seats when the train lurched forward. The sudden motion threw him off-balance, he grabbed one of the strap handles attached to a pole and hung on thinking, *What in the hell is Rubin doing?*

The train picked up more speed as it moved down the track. Paul panicked thinking Rubin was going to crash and they were going to be killed. He continued moving forward using the support straps like he was on a set of swinging monkey-bars. He reached the operator door and was shocked when Rubin opened it with a wide grin on his face.

Rubin turned his cap to the front and relaxed in the engineer's seat rocking back and forth in rhythm with the movement of the train. He was calm and in complete control as he drove the train like a seasoned professional. He navigated the green lights through the tunnel and maintained the train's speed while he checked the instrument panel. All Paul could do was take a seat for the ride.

Rubin passed two stations. There was no one waiting on the platforms until they approached the third station. Rubin slowly bought the train to a smooth stop at a red light and put on the brake. The police were waiting on the station platform with guns pointed at the train.

"Open the doors! Get off the train and put your hands up!"

Rubin waved at the police from the operator window, then flicked the correct switch to open the subway-train doors. He put his hands up with a big smile.

"Shiiiit Man, I've always wanted to drive this train. That was some cool shiiiit." Rubin extended his hand and offered Paul a high-five to confirm his accomplishment. Paul refused Rubin's hand, he was speechless.

Rubin walked proudly off the train and through the train doors. The five white policemen were unimpressed, but when they saw Paul stoop under the train doors to step off the train three of the cops stepped back and turned their weapons on Paul. The other two cops aimed at Rubin. Paul thought it was ironic that he escaped one gang just to be caught by another gang that was more dangerous and notorious.

One of the cops shouted, "Put your hands on your head and get on the floor!"

Rubin smiled then dropped to his knees and put his hands on top of the cap on his head. One of the cops holstered his gun to handcuff Rubin. The cop's voice was harsh and filled with hate. "Wipe that smile off your face Boy?" He slapped Rubin's face and Rubin's cap went flying off his head onto the train track. Rubin was silent but his smile was gone. The cop shouted in Rubin's face, "Boy who the fuck you think you are stealing a train? You think it's funny boy? You're in serious trouble!"

Paul's remained stone-faced but he felt a flood of emotions when he knelt down on the cold cement floor in front of the three cops pointing guns at him. He felt the steel of the handcuffs pinch as a cop restrained his large wrists; the sound of the metal locking into place shut down Paul's emotions and he turned cold. The officers backed away before he was ordered to stand up.

The Slapper cop pulled Rubin up from the floor. He flipped the back of Rubin's long hair; then, as if Rubin was a new species he identified, he announced to the other officers, "This is a Spic-Nigger." He spoke to Rubin in a menacing tone. "We're going to haul your ass down to the jailhouse. See what kind of trains you find inside a cell Boy!"

The other officers laughed at the innuendo. Rubin laughed too. Officer Slapper struck Rubin in the gut with his rubber club and pretended as if nothing happened. Paul saw all of the cops take pleasure in Rubin's pain and humiliation.

Officer Slapper gave orders to the other officers.

"Round their asses up and get em' in the wagon."

The other officers holstered their guns and pulled out their rubber clubs, then they motioned for Rubin and Paul to exit up the subway stairs.

Officer Slapper led the way up the steps and out of the subway station to a police van. He opened the back doors and said, "Get in! We gotta another ride for you Boys!"

One Phone Call

Paul and Rubin were separated when they arrived at the busy police station. One of the arresting officers told Paul he could make one phone call. He unlocked the handcuffs behind Paul's back then put them on again with Paul's hands shackled in the front. He stood behind Paul.

A desk officer with red hair, a pot-marked face and a pot belly to go with it slammed a dime down on the counter separating him from Paul. "We don't allow ya'll kind to use our phones! Go make your call over at the payphone." He pointed to the wall while the other officer waited to take Paul to a holding cell after the call.

Paul did as he was told. His wrists were hurt and bruised and his hands were still handcuffed, but without them pinned behind his back the blood circulation in his fingers started to return. He took the dime and walked over to one of the dirty pay-phones on the wall while the cop followed him.

It was awkward for Paul to place the dime in the pay slot with the pins and needles he felt in his fingers. He almost dropped it but he was finally able to push the coin into the narrow slot opening. He was relieved when the familiar jingle tone told him the deposit was accepted and he could dial. He called home hoping but also dreading his father would answer. His father answered on the second ring. He sounded sleepy and confused. "Hello... Paul? What time is it? Where are you?"

CharlesR was wide-awake after Paul explained his situation. He eased out of the bed without disturbing his wife. He held the phone close to his mouth and whispered, "Son are you downtown at the round-house?"

Paul's voice cracked when he responded, "Yes Sir."

CharlesR dressed quickly and quietly in the dark to avoid waking CoraLee. He crept down the hallway and woke Charles Jr. and Joseph. He kept his voice to a whisper while he explained. "I haveta go see about Paul. I don't know how much trouble he's in, but he's in jail and that's trouble enough. Charles Jr. get dressed, you're coming with me. Joey I need you to stay here with your mother and brothers."

Charles Jr. hurried to change out of his pajamas while CharlesR spoke to Joey.

"Joey, everybody's sleeping but when they wake up, don't tell them where we at. Tell them I said we'll be back shortly and to wash up and help your Mother with breakfast."

CharlesR grabbed his keys and put on his jacket; he was stern when he spoke to Joseph, "Tell your brothers to stay in the house til we get back." He gave Joseph a pat on the back and left with Charles Jr..

Consequences

CharlesR knew the Philadelphia police were racist and abusive; his main objective was to free his teenage son from the adult cage they put him in; he was furious but he maintained an outward calm. He parked in the public lot across from the police station. He told Charles Jr., "Lock the doors and stay in the car until we get back."

Charles Jr. was in distress but the look in his father's eyes put him at ease. He knew no matter the trouble Paul was in, his father was going to handle it. He waited for their return.

CharlesR was silent as he drove out of the public parking lot with both his sons. The sun was beginning to rise. Paul sat in the front passenger seat telling his father what happened during the night. Charles Jr. sat in the back seat listening to the incredible and scary story.

CharlesR finally broke his silence, his voice was like an unexpected thunderclap in the confines of the car. "Paul you're lucky you're alive!" CharlesR regained his composure before he spoke again. "Paul, they released you to me cause I know your rights. You're a minor. You were not operating the train but you could still be seen as an accomplice. Rubin is Black, eighteen and stole city property. They also found refer on him and the cops are saying he was high, laughing and smiling when they arrested him. His case is not going to go in his favor."

CharlesR reprimanded his son for being so foolish. "I taught you to be a leader. I thought you were a leader Paul." He stopped the car and looked Paul over from head to toe as if he did not know him. Paul hung his head down.

"Pick your head up son, you have no reason to hang your head. I want you to use this as a lesson for your future. Never make this mistake again; know what people are involved in before you go following behind them. Be your own man. Make good decisions because the consequences are far too great."

CharlesR took the long way home through the city park to educate his two eldest on what it meant to be a Black Man in a nation created, governed and dominated by White Men. He taught a Master Class in the time it took for them to reach home for breakfast. CharlesR reminded Paul and Charles Jr. about the history of enslavement and control and tied it to the continued oppression of the black population through the systemic laws. He told them in his final summary,

"The prison system is another extension of slavery

and oppression for us…modern Jim Crow. None of my sons are going to prison."

Man to Men Talk

The Ellison Boys were in the calm before the storm. A tornado was cycling overhead ready to touchdown at the kitchen table where they were summoned. CharlesR wanted all his sons to hear what led to Paul's predicament.

"Let me get this straight… you decided to go to a party with Rubin in a neighborhood known for gang-bangers and gang wars. There was a shootout at the party, you escaped, then Rubin stole a subway train and drove it through the subway tunnel in the middle of the night… no…wait…I should say early in the morning before rush hour…and after a few stops in the tunnel the cops were waiting with guns and took you and Rubin to jail. Did I get it straight?"

It was a rhetorical question, Paul was silent, everything his father said was shamefully true. There was a snicker from Peewee, it was silenced by a look from CharlesR signaling it was no laughing matter.

CharlesR rarely raised his voice or cursed but he was free to shout and use whatever colorful language he wanted because CoraLee was conveniently at the Five & Dime Store. She left the house so he could have his Man-to-Men talk with their sons. He started with Paul. "What the hell were you thinking Paul? You're smart son. Don't you see what's going on? Now you're in the court system, with a hearing, and ain't no telling what they going to do with your case!"

CharlesR paced around the kitchen as he spoke forcefully to his sons. "All y'all have grown up after the Civil Rights Movement. You think racial discrimination is outlawed but that's bull-shit! This country still has ways to enslave black people! Y'all still young and don't understand the unwritten rules yet. I'm telling you there is another movement...and the movement is for them to maintain power and control by keeping black people oppressed, uneducated, divided and weak-minded, especially black men!"

CharlesR's sons were paying attention to his every word. "Y'all represent the future of our race! The promise of something better. They are afraid of your power. Don't ya'll let them take away your power!"

CharlesR felt sad because Paul's poor decision would have repercussions on his future. He told him the facts. "Paul when you go into the court the judge is going to offer you the military or prison. You won't have no other choices cause they got the power over you now."

CharlesR spoke to his other sons, "Y'all listening and learning from this cause the military ain't for no black man and prison is worse!"

Charles Jr. was listening but he disagreed with his father about the military, he thought it was an honor to serve. He thought it was justified to defend the country you lived in; and if Paul had to enlist he was going to enlist too. Charles Jr. thought it was his choice to make not his father's; but he was not going to share his opinion or intentions while his father gave them another lecture.

Byron asked, "Can we go to court with Paul?"

CharlesR was firm, "No! Your mother is not going either."

Paul shifted in his chair but no one uttered a word. They waited to be dismissed.

"I'm tired," CharlesR said and walked out of the kitchen.

Mock Trial

Paul sat next to Rubin in the courtroom. This time he was totally aware of his situation. It did not take him long to see the trial was all for show. They were just going through the motions. A public defender was beside him and his father was seated in the front row behind them. There was no one present for Rubin. Recruitment representatives from four military branches were seated in the back row of the courtroom. There was never any mention Paul was a minor and the young white inexperienced public defender never challenged the legality of the inappropriate combined hearing; instead it was written into the court records Rubin Carlos Nieves and Paul Mansa Ellison were old enough to serve the country in a time of war.

Rubin and Paul were found guilty. Their crime carried a maximum prison sentence of ten years. The judge looked down at them from his high seat behind the bench. He spoke in a little squeaky voice. "I do not see the point in handing down the mandatory prison sentence to these able-bodied boys. These boys can be put to better use."

Rubin and Paul stood to hear the sentencing. They both faced the judge and looked him squarely in his eyes.

The judge turned red and sat up higher in his chair. He looked down at his papers when he pronounced the sentence. "To put your time and energy to better use, both of you will enlist in the military service by order of the court. Upon completion of your service prison sentences will be commuted." ...And just like that the judge ended the trial with a loud bang of the gavel.

Immediately after the proceedings, Rubin and Paul completed and signed military enlistment paperwork. Instructions were given with the date and time to report for induction into the service along with a bus station location and boarding time for the ride to bootcamp. They were released with a warning if they failed to report for induction arrest warrants would be immediately issued and they would serve the maximum prison sentence.

Goodbyes

CharlesR told the family Paul would say his goodbyes at home instead of the bus station. Charles Jr. pleaded with his father to accompany him with Paul; he said he wanted to say goodbye to Paul without his other brothers around; it was a pretense.

CharlesR discussed it with CoraLee and they agreed Charles Jr. could ride along. CoraLee ignored the protest from her other sons about the decision. She hugged, kissed and fussed over Paul and Charles Jr. and when they left she ran to the bedroom, closed the door and cried. Joey, Ronnie, Byron and Peewee sat in the living room in silence listening to their mother crying.

CharlesR parked at the end of the parking-lot far away from the bus station entrance. He wanted time with Paul away from the other families. He was hesitant before he stepped out of the car as he flashed back to the memory of his father sending him up North. He was seventeen then, Paul was the same age now and CharlesR was sending him down South. It was a full circle.

His voice was muffled by Paul's chest as he pulled hm into a hug trying to conceal his emotions. "I love you son. Watch your back." Paul dropped his head to his father's shoulder and his father reached up to pat his back. Paul said, "I love you too Pop. I'll do my best." They separated to exchange their special handshake.

Charles Jr. watched the exchange with a smile; his smile turned into a grimace when Paul stood aside and pushed him toward his father. CharlesR opened his arms and embraced Charles Jr.. His heartache doubled but it was also filled with pride knowing his first born son had the confidence to make his own decision. "I love you," they said at the same time, then Charles Jr. exchanged his own special handshake with his father.

CharlesR took a long look at his sons standing side by side. His boys were evolving into men. He guided them into a circle; they held hands and bowed their heads in prayer. CharlesR prayed his sons would not be destroyed before they reached full manhood then he got back into the car to return home.

Paul and Charles Jr. watched their father drive out of the parking lot before they walked into the bus station. Rubin was already waiting inside puffing on a cigarette. He was holding an open seat with his jacket. He did not seem surprised to see Charles Jr. with Paul. He threw his bag across another empty seat and grinned at the Ellison

Brothers. He told them, "Shiiiit, these motherfuckers gonna cut off my hair."

January 1968 Charles Randolph Ellison Jr., eighteen; Paul Mansa Ellison seventeen; and Rubin Carlos Nieves, eighteen; were inducted into the United States Marine Corps. It was one of the most turbulent years in America.

In 1968 Martin Luther King Jr. and Robert F. Kennedy were assassinated. Antiwar activists and other demonstrators including groups like the Students for a Democratic Society and the Black Panthers showed up in Chicago during the Democratic Convention. The television stations were broadcasting racial unrest and the police brutality against peaceful protestors. Two Black Men, recipients of olympic gold and bronze metals in track and field, raised a gloved fist in protest during the metal ceremony as the U. S. national anthem was played. Richard Nixon became the president of the United States by a' narrow victory. The end of the same year, on Christmas eve, three U. S. astronauts orbited the moon ten times.

Vietnam

The pain was agonizing. Paul's feet felt like thousands of bugs were gnawing away at his toes. He clutched his rifle but he could not see because his eyes were teary and burning from the sweet smelling mustard gas. He closed his eyes and when he opened them again he stared into the red bulging eyes of a yellow fish. It hovered in front him slightly above his head. It swam back-and-forth in the air then started to speak. Paul smelled its hot breath as incoherent words fell from its mouth; it was a horrid smell like burning flesh; and something else lingered as the yellow fish exhaled breath into the air. It was a faint sweet aromatic smell, like the wood-chips his father used on the barbecue grill. It was a pleasant scent mingled with all the other odors. He also smelled chicken noodle soup.

Paul did not trust his senses. He walked for days after the Vietnamese army and Guerrilla soldiers ambushed his platoon. Paul witnessed carnage he could never have imagined. Men he bathed with; slept with; ate with; joked with; gambled with; laughed with; cried with and bled with were blown into bloody mangled pieces all around him. Explosive mortar shells, land mines and booby-traps were the weapons the Viet Cong used against the U. S. soldiers without mercy. Paul's platoon was not outgunned, they were outwitted.

Paul did what he was trained to do, he fought for his life and killed as many as he could before what was left of his platoon was ordered to retreat. The ambush severed communications and separated the troop. Paul crawled over the dead bodies covering the ground. He could not tell the difference between the American and Viet Cong soldiers but he recognized all the human body parts.

Embers and ash were carried on the wind while American soldiers in rubber waders, rubber boots, rubber gloves and gas masks set fires to the fields. Paul tore a part off his uniform and wrapped it around his nose and mouth. He headed toward the marsh and stayed low to keep from choking on the fumes and smoke. He walked then crawled through the thick swamp following the voices in his head until the yellow fish with its big red eyes appeared and started swimming around him again. Paul thought he was dying.

Saigon

Han Vo's father, Chin Vo was a North Vietnamese patriot in the service of the Emperor Bảo Đại. His mother, Yan, was a South Vietnamese woman, she married Chin while he was stationed in Saigon. Han knew his father and mother had substantial wealth after they were married but Han never saw any of it. His parents were stripped of their wealth and removed from their home by the North Vietnamese and the Democratic Republic of Vietnam also known as the DRV.

Forced into exile, his father took his mother to her parent's home. Chin and Yan Vo made a new home in South Vietnam where Han was born. Han studied hard in school. He was smart and he learned languages easily; by the time he was a teenager he could speak five; Vietnamese, Chinese, Mandarin, French and English. Han dreamed of becoming a physician and traveling the world to practice medicine. Han's dreams were deferred.

The National Liberation Front was a political organization in South Vietnam and Cambodia. The Front with its own army was fighting South Vietnam and the United States. They falsely claimed Han's father Chin was a counter revolutionary helping the United States and his mother Yan was a co-conspirator. Chin Vo was publicly beheaded and Yan Vo was taken away to a prison camp. Han suspected his mother was murdered and buried in one of the mass graves the Communist reserved for the people. The authorities removed Han from school and turned him over to his grandparents. Han's grandparents never spoke a word of any of it, they were living in fear for their own lives.

Han now a young man of twenty, saw the world changing all around them, he knew they were no longer safe in Saigon so he made plans to leave. He heard only the Americans were being evacuated. His sources were random survivors and he hoped it was not true. He was aware the planes stopped flying into the airport but he still saw the U. S. helicopters hovering and occasionally landing. The helicopter exhaust fumes were thick and the spinning steel propellers forced the air down and flattened the fields. It stilled the sway of rice plants, killing what Han's people called the "sóng lúa." Daily chemical spraying killed the forestation. Han's people suffered from the chemical fallout in the air. Fresh food was scarce and water was not fit to use without boiling it. Many of the vulnerable did not survive. Han's grandparents perished, there was nothing he could do to save them.

Han Vo was the lone survivor of his family and his village. The picturesque blue skies above green rolling hills and fragrant poppied fields of Saigon turned into smoke filled skies over a fire-bombed war zone. The Saigon River ran red with the blood of his countrymen.

Han was able to scrounge for food. He discovered the abandoned Củ Chi tunnels, used by Viet Cong soldiers on one of his excursions. There were plenty of supplies left behind including clean water. He took what he needed. He crawled through the tunnels to make his way up the river undetected then he built a hidden shelter close to the tunnels to rest.

Han saw the American soldier while he was scouting. He was the biggest Black man Han had ever seen. He watched the big solider stumble through the marsh groaning with each step, talking to himself, picking up and dropping large rocks. The solider stopped abruptly and stood still looking into the air. Han was cautious as he approached the tall American solider and looked up into his face. His dark skin was covered in green paint and his lips were cracked from dehydration.

His eyes were vacant as he stared ahead at nothing. The solider was in shock. Han was familiar with the symptoms, he saw soldiers on both sides of the conflict disoriented with expressions devoid of emotion. The big solider fell forward and Han caught him. Han was strong but he struggled with the height and bulk of the huge man.

Han dragged the solider out of the marsh and was soaking wet and drenched in sweat by the time he laid him down outside his secret hideaway. Han went inside his hut, removed his boots, stripped his wet clothes off and dipped his feet into a pan of filtered water. He dried off his body and feet with straw and a fine blue powder before he put on dry clothes and stepped into straw slippers.

The American solider was still semi-conscious when Han returned to check his condition. Han put one of the two gas masks over the soldier's face he took from the supplies in the tunnels. He checked over the solider's body for wounds but found no serious injuries. He pulled off the solider's waterlogged boots and the foul and putrid smell was overpowering. Han put on the other gas mask. He removed the solider's fungus encrusted socks being careful not to pull off any of his skin. He examined the soldier's feet. They were almost unrecognizable, bloody, swollen and full of infection. Han did not know how the solider was able to walk.

Han relit the fire under his pots and mixed the herbs he collected along his journey. The preparation would not cure the big soldier's ailment, but Han knew how to abate the skin to avoid further infection and ease the man's suffering. It would be left up to a real doctor to repair the damage. Han pulled his mask aside when he was finished then pulled the soldier's mask aside too and waited for him to wake from his sleep.

Hours passed while Han sat waiting quietly by the fire until he heard the sound of the solider stirring. The solider sat straight up and clutched his rifle. Han raised his hands and spoke English. "I am Han, a friendly, not part of this war. You are hurt. Rest, eat, drink then we must move on." Han knew if he could get the American solider to the U. S. evacuation site it would be his own ticket out of Saigon. Han held his hands up higher and pointed toward the fields to assure the solider he meant no harm. "We can help each other," he said.

The American soldier did not lift his head to see

the fires glowing in the distance. He slumped back to the ground, clutched his rifle tighter and closed his eyes again. Han cautiously placed the mask back over the solider's face.

Alive

Paul sopped up his second bowl of broth with a rice cake that melted in his mouth when it touched his tongue. It was the best meal he had in months, far better than the military rations of salty spam in a can and stale peanut butter sandwiches. He was starting to feel better with clean drinking water and warm food in his stomach; and whatever the Vietnamese man put on his feet was working. Despite the pasty, gooey feeling on his skin under the thick wrappings the itching stopped and his pain diminished. Paul felt alive again and he was able to breathe without choking. Two hot bowls of the broth cleared his head and gave him energy. He slurped up the rest of the liquid and tried to ignore the distant sounds of rapid fire and explosions.

Fires were glowing around the land under a beautiful night sky with a curtain of twinkling stars. Paul looked away from the sky choosing instead to look at the fire under the pot. The pot was suspended by thick bamboo poles over a bundle of red rocks that looked like handmade coal. Paul thought the cooking fire was a simple but genius design. He could smell the liquid inside the pot as it began to boil. It was a pleasant. The little

Vietnamese man squatted down on his haunches over the boiling mixture and dropped leaves into the pot. His movements were graceful as he stretched back and forth between the pot and a large flat rock covered with straw he used as a table. He picked up a thick bamboo stick. Paul checked his rifle resting against his leg.

Han saw Paul's movements but pretended not to notice. He moved back to the pot and used the stick to push the leaves deep down under the scalding hot liquid. He stirred the mixture slowly with the bamboo and turned his head slightly to avoid inhaling the vapors the leaves released as they wilted into the mix.

Paul's head felt heavy and smoke from the pot blurred his vision. The little Vietnamese man moved in and out of focus. Paul thought he saw the man sink into the ground but when his vision cleared the little man was kneeling by his side taking away the empty bowl. Paul accepted the hot cup he offered. He took a sip of the liquid and the little man encouraged him to inhale the steam. Paul inhaled the steam floating above the cup. Colors exploded in his head. The man helped him stand and miraculously Paul felt like he was walking on clouds.

California

Charles Jr. watched television in the mess-hall. It was a time of protest against the Vietnam war. American citizens were grief stricken about the number of lives lost from all three branches of the military. They were tired of seeing their boys come home in boxes, they wanted their boys to come home to dinner. There was the shooting of a protesting college student captured in photos too graphic for words. The photos were released and it tipped the scales of public opinion.

After serving his country for four years Charles Jr. was returning home. An honorable discharge paper and transport pass were in his pocket. He shoved the last of his belongings in his duffel bag then surveyed the empty barracks. The California base was in a celebratory mood but Charles was not. He was uneasy and worried about his brother.

A year had passed since their last letter exchange. Paul's last letter was filled with complimentary descriptions of Japan, Okinawa and Saigon. He complained about the heat, the jungle, the barracks and the military rations. He wrote about a friendly Vietnamese village and his experience in their clubs. He described a few encounters with the Vietnamese women but left out details. He wrote about the quirks of the brothers who were his friends. He asked about the weather and beaches in California. He asked about the family and ended with personal messages for Chay to deliver whenever his leave was granted. Paul never wrote about the war or his combat duties.

Charles Jr. never saw combat. He saw soldiers return from deployments missing limbs or their wits. Their faces were aged beyond their years, boys prematurely turned into men by the war experience. Some of the boy-men suffered silently; while some raged at anyone who was close or foolish enough to become a target; some wanted to go back to war to finish killing. Charles Jr. prayed for Paul every time he heard word of heavy casualties. He prayed Paul was still alive no matter his condition.

Charles Jr. called home. His father answered and his mother joined on the other extension. He was happy to hear their voices. He heard his boisterous brothers in the background until his mother told them to be quiet. They had no news about Paul so Charles Jr. focused on his own good news. He told them he was coming home.

At Home

There were rumors the military draft was going to end. Richard Nixon was a second-term president who lied to the nation in the past and CharlesR did not trust the tricky U. S. president and his promises. The public labeled him, 'Tricky Dick,' CharlesR thought the name was appropriate.

CharlesR was angry his sons were forced to serve in a war that made no sense to him. He wanted both his sons home. The last time he saw Charles Jr. and Paul was at the bootcamp graduation when the entire family traveled south to attend. It was bitter sweet seeing his sons in uniforms marching in formation across the field.

As soon as the family returned to Philadelphia, CharlesR started writing letters to his sons. It took a while for the responses to arrive, but his letters were answered. The letters revealed they each were experiencing very different military lives. CharlesR read in-between the lines and saw the invisible words his sons did not write on the pages. He was proud of their maturity in handling their individual situations. Charles Jr. was moved around the country from one military base to another making his way up the ranks. Paul was deployed overseas for a year of combat duty; he was fighting on another continent nine thousand miles away.

Meanwhile, the Ellison family was engaged in a fight at home for their own rights and CharlesR made sure his other four sons stayed out of trouble. He kept track of their every move, it was not easy with four teenagers but with CoraLee as his partner they managed. CoraLee was vigilant about schoolwork, but CharlesR also expected the boys to participate in extra curricular activities. CoraLee laid out the schedule for homework, chores and errands. CharlesR made sure his sons learned how to make house repairs. He took them to assist him with his growing renovation business. He took time during the projects to have more talks. There was no down-time for the Ellisons boys.

Joey, Ronnie and Byron were good students. Joey was exceptional in biological sciences. Ronnie excelled in math and Byron was a great debater. Peewee, inspired by music, declared he was a musician. Peewee learned piano then mastered every other instrument he tried.

CharlesR and CoraLee's goal was to get their boys through high-school and into good colleges. The Vietnam War provided extra motivation because college students were entitled to a deferment from the military. If the boys were enrolled in college it meant they would be classified as '2-S Status' and exempt from the draft; if they dropped out or stopped making progress in community college before transferring to a four-year college or graduating they were still subject to the military draft.

Joseph, Ronald and Byron were enrolled in separate colleges pursuing different studies. Joseph had a full ride to a Historic Black University to study medicine. Scholarships, profits from the construction business and donations from family and church members helped with Ronald and Byron's tuition. Ronald did not officially declare his major but Byron was leaning toward psychology. Peewee, who now preferred to be called Gene, was a senior in high-school. Gene acquired early acceptance into the Philadelphia Music Academy with a promise for a fellowship. CharlesR and CoraLee achieved their goal.

Chapter Three
ELLISONS - The Aftermath

America & Vietnam

Nixon's impeachment was underway after he was caught on tape for the crimes he continually denied. The Vietnam War was ending but the number of African-American soldiers still being killed was alarming. Charles Jr. and Paul were both honorably discharged after serving four and a half years in the marines. CharlesR was cheerful as he ushered Charles Jr. and Paul though the house to the backyard.

"How's Mom?" Charles Jr. asked.

"She'll be better now that y'all back home." CharlesR gave Charles Jr. a pat on his back. He was happy his whole family was together. "Y'all look good! Paul you got muscles on top of muscles. Your Mother is going to flip a bird when she sees how big y'all got…and your brothers…wait til y'all see how much they've grown… even Peewee, I mean Gene," he said with a chuckle.

Charles Jr. and Paul were given a 'Heroes Welcome' with a big family celebration. Joseph, Byron, Ronald and Gene celebrated their older brothers with cheers, their favorite foods and plenty of beer. CharlesR and CoraLee celebrated the return of their sons alive and in one piece. The rest of the country had mixed feelings about the returning Vietnam Veterans.

The Vietnam War was televised and for the first time ordinary American citizens saw from an eye-level view the actual combat, destruction and death of the war. The anti-war protest grew stronger and ironically some protesters blamed the war on the soldiers who were forced to fight it. Nixon's fiasco, exposure of his crimes and impeachment forced him to resign. President Ford, Nixon's former vice president, granted Nixon a full and unconditional pardon for all crimes he might have committed against the United States as president. The pardon covered Nixon's actions during the scandal known as Watergate. In a nationally televised broadcast President Ford said it was in the best interest for the nation. A year later Ford signed an executive order and announced the evacuation of all the American civilians and military personnel in Saigon, along with tens of thousands of South Vietnamese civilians associated with the southern regime. He went on television and promised they would be protected by U. S. security forces. Ford said, the plan was to airlift military personnel, American citizens and Vietnam refugees offshore for military pick up and further assignment. It was a forgone conclusion the capital of South Vietnam would fall under the power the People's Army of Vietnam and the National Liberation

Front. The 1975 event marked the end of the Vietnam War and the start of a transition period eventually leading to the formal reunification of Vietnam under communist rule.

CoraLee was relieved when the war was finally declared over. Her sons were her heroes no matter the outcome because they survived. She was no longer distressed but she could see the military and the war irrevocably changed her two eldest sons. The military turned her boys into men yet they suffered like children from emotions they were not equipped to handle. CoraLee knew the guilt, remorse, anger and sadness they felt caused invisible wounds. She put her energy into helping them heal from their trauma. CoraLee's heart ached especially for Paul.

Adjustments

Charles Jr. appreciated the welcome home from his family but the whole notion of being celebrated as a hero made him feel sick to his stomach. The soldiers who fought and survived; the P.O.Ws (prisoners of war); the M.I.A (missing in action); and the K.I.A. (killed in action) were the real heroes as far as Charles Jr. was concerned. Charles Jr. was never in the real war. Family and friends thought Charles Jr. was lucky but he thought because he was the eldest, the military should have deployed him to Vietnam instead of Paul. Charles Jr. tried to trade places with Paul. He inquired about the matter only to be told Paul volunteered for overseas combat duty when he enlisted. Every time his younger brothers would ask him about his military experiences Charles Jr. would think about Paul the real hero. His brothers did not have a clue that compared to Paul Charles Jr. had it easy. Meanwhile, Paul was avoiding him. Charles Jr. understood his brother was only trying to adjust in his own way, but it still hurt not being able to talk to Paul.

Outside the Ellison circle Charles Jr. was just another unemployed Black man in America; no one respected or cared about his veteran status. He kept to himself and began to slowly withdraw from his family. He left the house each day and took long walks through the neighborhood. He rode downtown on the city trolleys and buses of the expanded public transportation system. The city had grown in the four years he was away. Charles spent hours wandering around looking at the new construction and unfamiliar high-rise buildings.

Repercussions

The Vietnam War haunted Paul. His foot pain was chronic and it would continually plague him for the rest of his life. He was grateful he still had two feet thanks to Han and his friendship. Paul's body could have recovered from something nature inflicted but it was man who caused his life-time of misery. The government advisors said, 'Agent Orange' was the military's ally in the Vietnam War; it thinned out the jungle to make ground warfare possible in terrain unfamiliar to U. S. soldiers. They did not tell the soldiers it was a toxic biohazard. They did not tell the U. S. soldiers after they sprayed humans would also rot like the jungle. The government told everyone the chemicals were harmless to human life.

Chemicals from U. S. spray boats and trucks traveled over the military zones. Orange smoke drifted down from the planes. Soldiers breathed in and walked through the saturated terrain. The side-effects Paul experienced along with thousands of other U. S. soldiers revealed a terrible truth. The government approved and unloaded deadly toxins on its own soldiers and they were slowly poisoned. Paul never imagined after the sacrifice and heroism from his comrades, their own government would be their undoing. Like many other Vietnam Veterans, Paul filed a class-action law suit against the chemical companies. He submitted claims for compensation from the Department of Veteran Affairs; but there was nothing that could compensate Paul for his constant physical pain or his psychological trauma. He searched for something to numb his pain, erase his memories and quell his nightmares. Paul turned to drugs.

Future Forward

CharlesR was worried about his two eldest sons. Charles Jr. and Paul were never present and he could not keep track of their whereabouts. Charles Jr. spent days out the house returning only to eat with the family and help with chores. Paul slept during the day then spent evenings and late nights out in the streets. CharlesR decided he would have them focus on the family business to get them back on track. He put a plan together, consulted with CoraLee and put the plan into action.

The fall semester started and Joseph, Byron, Ronald and Gene were back in school. It was a busy season for the construction business and there was a long list of projects.

CharlesR delegated some of the projects to Charles Jr. and Paul. He assigned them repair jobs and told them to fix the houses together by the dates on the contract and to give him regular updates. CharlesR was brilliant. His plan provided a safe environment for his sons to talk alone and reconnect with each other. The small jobs with families gave each of them time to decompress and adjust to being back home until they felt comfortable reintegrating into the larger community. It kept them productive and they became appreciative of the work. It gave CharlesR an opportunity to keep an eye on his grown sons while respecting their manhood.

CharlesR took time training and teaching them about the business trade and the process of renovation and construction. The business grew over the years and CharlesR was adamant about doing each job right and respecting the customers he called 'clients.'

Charles Jr. and Paul followed every instruction their father gave. They collaborated to solve problems and figured out who was best at each task. Charles Jr. was best at working directly with clients to understand the project. Paul suggested Charles Jr. use his nick-name 'Chay' so clients would not confuse him with their father. Paul worked well with the suppliers and made sure materials matched specifications. They were both good builders, they were taught by a master and had a lot of practice at home and in the community. Business discussions between them came naturally and in the months that followed they became close brothers again. They played pranks on one other in between the work, shared jokes, laughed and smiled more often. They enjoyed running the small projects together and reporting their progress to their father.

Chay and Paul worked tirelessly and eventually their efforts showed in the work they completed. All the clients were happily satisfied and the financial results were profitable. The Ellison Brothers were building on the stellar reputation CharlesR established. CharlesR congratulated Chay and Paul on their success.

Ellison Christmas

The Ellison Christmas of 1976 was the first time in five years all of the Ellisons were together for the holiday season. Philadelphia was covered in a soft blanket of winter snow. It was cold but the sun was shining. It felt like the old days before the war and civil unrest. Folks greeted each other with smiles while Christmas shopping, the Ellisons were no exception.

CoraLee drove her new red hatch-back car to shop for groceries not available from her husband's greenhouse. The Ellison men took the old station wagon and new truck to buy one of biggest Christmas trees that would fit in the house. Christmas Eve day everyone spent the day at home decorating, cooking and tasting. Christmas Day they headed to early church service. It was an uplifting spiritual celebration and after the service the Ellisons were acknowledged by the church community. The Ellisons returned home exchanged gifts and watched movies on the television until dinner time.

The formal dinning room table was set, the food was blessed and the holiday meal was ready. It was a feast fit for a King, his Queen and the six Princes. CharlesR and CoraLee sat at opposite ends of the table flanked by three sons on each side. The room was filled with jovial discussions while holiday music favorites played on Gene's new stereo. The stereo was a gift from Paul. He asked Han to ship it from his new home in Japan. Gene was disappointed when his mother was noncommittal about allowing him to take the stereo with him to the academy. He got over his disappointment when Paul surprised him with a portable electric keyboard too.

Charles Jr. and Paul were happy their younger brothers were home for the holidays. Joseph and Byron were eager to share stories about campus life. Ronald talked about an investment program he joined and Gene talked about the new ways technology was changing and evolving music industry.

CharlesR looked at his large family, his beautiful home and the abundant meal. He was struck by how far he traveled with one suit, one suitcase, a few dollars and seeds in his pocket to end up at his own dining table eating some of foods grown from those very seeds with a new generation. He realized in that moment the future his father dreamed for the Ellison family came to fruition. He cleared his throat to make an announcement. "Now that all you guys are here together, I want to discuss the future. I want y'all to take a look at the plans I have for our construction business. You know I'm not getting any younger."

Gene interrupted, "Pop don't worry you know Dr. Joey will take care of you."

CharlesR laughed then turned serious. "Listen up cause this is important. I want to make sure there's something for y'all to hand down to your children and your Mother says if I don't spend more time at *this* house I'm going to be living in the next house I fix." There was hearty laughter around the table.

CoraLee smiled at CharlesR from the opposite end of the formal dining table. The distance between them shortened when he returned her smile. Then he turned his attention back to his sons. He pointed to the oldest two and to everyone's surprise except his wife he announced, "Charles Jr. and Paul will take lead of the new Ellison Construction and Renovation business. We're going to form a partnership with Charles Jr. and Paul in charge of projects and business operations. I'm expecting all of you to contribute to the success of the business. Your education and talents will determine your roles."

CharlesR could tell his sons thought it was a great idea by the way they were nodding their approval. They all wanted to be a part of the family business.

Charles Jr. spoke to his younger brothers. "Yeah, your studies come first…but believe me we're going to need your help with stuff."

Paul spoke with his mouth full of food. "I didn't know der was so much work to the biz..ness." CoraLee gave Paul a disapproving frown. He swallowed his food and wiped his mouth on a holiday dinner napkin before he spoke again.

"I mean it's more than just fixing and building stuff. There's a lot of moving parts in this business and Pops been teaching us a lot, but we're gonna be more successful with all of y'all getting those degrees."

Paul punched Joseph in his arm playfully. "Dr. Joey you better finish school quick, cause we're gonna need a doctor on site the way Chay swings a hammer!"

More laughter ensued before CharlesR spoke again. "We're going to make sure we have our licenses and legal paperwork in order and make this business official." He raised his glass and waited for everyone else to do the same.

Cora-Lee raised her glass and rose from her chair. Everyone stood up when the Queen left her seat. CoraLee spoke softly to the grown men she raised.

"You're brothers are right, your education will allow all of you to compete in this world and contribute to the business, so stay focused and when you are ready you can join in." CoraLee looked lovingly at her husband. "Your father is also right, it's time for him to slow down. Your older brothers are ready to run the business." She raised her glass to make a toast. "I'm proud of all of my Princes. My Six Towers! Merry Christmas!" She winked at her husband and took a sip of eggnog. CharlesR thought his wife summed it up nicely.

Two Hearts

The new year came and the frigid northeast winter settled over the city. CoraLee caught the flu; she recovered but her health still seemed affected. She ate very little and was not her usual energetic self. CharlesR thought it was because the boys returned to their schools and Chay and Paul were busy all the time with jobs outside the house; in his heart he knew his wife's decline came from the accumulation of stress and worry.

CoraLee saw soldiers retuning home from the war as amputees or worst, inside military caskets. She prayed with the families of the young boys listed missing in action. She remained strong throughout the entire ordeal. It was a heavy load for his Queen so CharlesR tried to carry some of the weight at home as his sons took on more of the business.

In February of 1977 while he was in his greenhouse gathering flowers to give CoraLee for Valentine's Day, Charles Randolph Ellison suffered a fatal heart attack.

CharlesR was the only heir of his deceased parents Randolph and Beulah Ellison. He owned the farmhouse in Savanah with acres of farmland and the family burial plots. He owned his beautifully renovated Philadelphia home and a profitable construction business. He left a Will and substantial life insurance. CharlesR was thorough. CoraLee inherited all her husband's property and wealth with provisions set aside for each son. She asked Charles Jr. to act as the executor of his father's estate.

The Ellison family decided the funeral services would take place in Philadelphia and the burial down south. CharlesR would be interred on the farm in Georgia next to his father, mother and older brother Randolph Jr. in accordance with his will. CoraLee had mixed emotions about her husband's resting place being so far away from their home in Philadelphia. She was comforted after her sons promised they would take her down south to visit whenever she wanted.

CharlesR's death was sudden and it was a shock to the Ellison family. The Ellison Brothers remembered their father's words about strength and unity and their mother's words about being tested. They were all being tested and if the Ellisons could get through the loss of the head of their family together they knew they could get through anything.

The following spring, CoraLee began to exhibit

signs of depression. Byron and Gene tried to keep her spirits up. Joseph checked on her physical health while Chay took her to church. Ron bought her groceries and Chay cooked meals on occasions when the hired cook was off. They all made sure she ate regularly and took walks. Things turned for the worst by the heat of the summer when CoraLee stopped going to church and socializing. She experienced severe mood swings and refused to talk to her friends. She remained in her bedroom reading from the bible or looking through scrap books and the photo albums she pulled out of the old cedar wood chest.

Chay reached out to his brothers to discuss their mother's condition and decide the best approach for her care. It was a difficult discussion but together the brothers took their mother to the hospital for evaluation and treatment.

CoraLee fought all the way. She cursed at them and told them if their father was alive they wouldn't lock her up. She spat at them and banished them from her kingdom. She said they would burn in hell for locking their mother in a dungeon. She declared she would escape and find their father to punish them. Then she touched Chay's dimpled chin and spoke to him as if he were her dead husband. "I love you, I thought you left me but you came back. Tell them I don't want to go to jail. I'm innocent." She cried in confusion, "What's wrong with me? I don't understand what's happening? Why are y'all doing this to me?" CoraLee's sons knew it was the dementia talking but it did not lessen the pain of seeing their mother act completely out of character.

It was as if CoraLee needed to escape her husband's death. Her mind took her to a place where her sons could not visit. She was not prepared to live in a world without her beloved husband. Although her faith told her CharlesR was in a better place she was never the same after his death. Her grief plunged her into a pool of deep depression. Her sons tried to help her through it, sometimes she remembered them, sometimes she did not. Gradually CoraLee lost her will to fight her mind's journey. She traveled along until she joined her husband. She died in the winter on a snowy Sunday afternoon. The Ellison Brothers believed a broken heart was the cause of their mother's death not the Alzheimer's disease. They buried their mother on the Ellison farmland next to their father.

Chapter Four
CHARLES - Ready or Not

Joelle

Joelle's teacher Miss Kimble explained the reason for the special parent teacher conference. "Mr. and Mrs. Duemijon, Joelle completes all assignments ahead of her peers and she achieves an 'A' on every assignment. I recommend we move her up to the next grade level. I believe she can do the work."

Joelle's parents were hesitant because Joelle skipped the first grade, skipping two grades was a big leap. Mrs. Duemijon was concerned the move might be too much. She did not want Joelle ridiculed by older children or disappointed if it did not work out. Mr. Duemijon thought his six-year old little girl was too young to be in the same class with eight and nine-year old children.

Miss Kimble was empathetic. "I know you're concerned but I really believe Joelle can handle the work and the challenge will make her happier."

Miss Kimble persuaded the Duemijons to allow Joelle to skip to the third grade. The Duemijons agreed because they wanted their child to be happy.

Joelle was able to complete her assignments with straight 'A's' in her new third grade class. She had the admiration of teachers but she did not have friends.

One day Dr. Mortimer visited her classroom. He was a tall thin white man with the thick eyeglasses. His eyes blinked constantly while he read over his notes. He administered a series of tests to the entire third grade class and said he would return with the results.

A month later the Duemijons received a phone call from the school principal requesting a meeting. The call set off alarm bells. The Duemijons thought there was something seriously wrong. They were afraid that giving permission to place Joelle in third grade was a mistake.

The family arrived early for the meeting. A teacher's assistant escorted them into the teacher's lounge. She ushered Joelle to a seating area filled with children's books and educational magazines. Joelle's parents took seats at a table and waited nervously for the principal to arrive.

Ms. Saunders, Joelle's new third grade teacher arrived first. She said hello to Joelle and shook hands with the Duemijons. Ms. Saunders said with great enthusiasm,

"Principal Brooks is on his way. We're so pleased you agreed to meet with us today."

A few minutes later Principal Brooks entered the teacher's lounge accompanied by two men he introduced as social scientists, Dr. Mortimer and Mr. Farber. He thanked everyone for coming then asked them to be seated. He spoke highly of his teachers and Joelle before he turned the meeting over to Dr. Mortimer.

Joelle listened to the adults discuss her as if she was not in the room.

Dr. Mortimer spoke rapidly like he was reading from a script. "I study the distribution of IQ scores in populations across the city and compare the relationships between the IQ score and other variables. IQ scores are used as predictors of educational achievement or special needs."

Mrs. Duemijon looked worried. Mr. Duemijon looked angry. He was insulted a stranger tested his daughter without his knowledge and had the nerve to say they was not providing what Joelle needed. He did not trust the fast talking white man.

Dr. Mortimer was oblivious to the Duemijon's negative reaction. He looked proud like he discovered something rare and extraordinary. He announced with a little fanfare and unexpected showmanship, "Joelle Deliore Duemijon is a validated genius! All the test scores indicated she is an exceptional learner. We've determined Joelle has an innate, personal aptitude for abstract thought and superior skills in understanding; communicating; reasoning; learning and problem solving!"

Ms. Saunders smiled at Joelle. She touched Mrs. Duemijon's hand and told her, "Mrs. Duemijon we're excited for Joelle! You should be excited too! This will open up opportunities for her. It's a good thing."

Principal Brooks was in agreement too, he was smiling proudly at Joelle from his seat at the table. Mrs. Duemijon's expression turned to relief but Mr. Duemijon's expression did not change. He was not convinced it was a good thing, it sounded like more gibberish to him.

Mr. Farber spoke slower than Dr. Mortimer. "Yes Ms. Saunders is correct this is a good thing. In fact, it's a GREAT thing. It's wonderful news. Your daughter's intelligence classification is high on both the…Terman's Stanford-Binet and Wechsler's charts…with her scores she can enroll at a special school free of cost."

Mr. Farber took a folder out of his briefcase and pushed it across the table to the Duemijons. The Duemijons opened the folder and turned through pages of reports filled with graphs and numbers documenting Joelle's high IQ test results. The only things Mr. and Mrs. Duemijon understood in the reports were Joelle's name, date of birth and social security number.

Joelle sat in the big chair in the corner quietly reading. Mr. Farber turned his chair around to ask Joelle, "Would you like to go to a new school with other children that learn as fast as you?"

Joelle closed the educational digest magazine and placed it on the table. Ms. Saunders told her she was very smart and a quick learner. She did not need to read her reports. The fact of the matter was, because Joelle was intellectually gifted, she understood the results of her test scores better than anyone in the room. Joelle heard and understood everything Dr. Mortimer tried to convey to her parents. Joelle felt Mr. Farber genuinely believed he could help, she was also gifted with superior instincts. She liked Mr. Farber. His furry white mustache moved up and down when he spoke and it made her laugh.

Joelle, in her soft spoken articulate child's voice, answered with a question. "Does the school have books with different math problems and puzzles?" She did not wait for Mr. Farber to answer she continued to talk. "Because I like books, math and putting puzzles together.... I have puzzles at home... I figure them out too easy though...Do you like puzzles?... They make nice gifts...My Nans gave me one for my fifth birthday but I lost two pieces. My Nans spoke a different language!" She paused and seemed sad for a moment but then she finished her story. "I still put it together because I saw what it looked liked from the picture on the box...then Mommy and Daddy bought me a bigger puzzle." Joelle spread her little brown arms wide to show the size of the puzzle. "I didn't lose any pieces to that one. I put the big puzzle together fast too...didn't I Mommy?" She glanced at her mother but she did not wait for confirmation about her puzzle skills. She kept talking as she tried to make her feet touch the floor while sitting in the grown up chair. "Then I took the big puzzle apart and put it back together again faster...I like the big puzzle......It's a map of the United States of America...Do you know all the united states in America? Oooh, I can tell you and I can spell out the names...I can tell you the date each state was ratified too...if you want to know...if you don't know already." She looked innocently at Mr. Farber.

The adults were astonished when Joelle proceeded to name each state and its corresponding ratification date. After she named ten states, her mother gave her a signal they heard enough, so Joelle asked other questions about the school. She wanted to know if the teachers spoke or taught other languages and if there was a recess. She asked if the new school had a lunchroom and if she had to eat every food they served. She frowned and said she did not like beets, then she let out a big yawn.

Mrs. Duemijon apologized. "I'm sorry but it's close to Jo's nap time." It was a reminder to the other adults the genius in the room was a six-year old.

The Duemijons were well aware their daughter was special before experts confirmed with test results. They witnessed Joelle's intelligence from the day she was born. She proved in nursery school she was far more advanced than the other children. Now in primary school she showed how easily and quickly she could learn and retain information. A new school where Joelle could explore her talents without boundaries was a gift. Her parents thought a school with children like Joelle would be a better fit. It was important for her future education; but more importantly her mother and father wanted Joelle to develop into a healthy and content adult. They could not stand in the way of her opportunity. Manuela and Dane Duemijon agreed to enroll Joelle in the Philadelphia School for the Gifted. Her father warned everyone if he saw any signs his little girl was unhappy they would have to deal with him.

Joelle transitioned smoothly into the new school. She loved mathematics, languages and history and with an IQ over 150 she excelled. She read at least three books at a time and finished them within a week. She joined the Book Club and the Math Club. She made new friends.

Joelle discovered her passion early; at fifteen she decided she wanted to be a teacher. She enjoyed learning and discovering new information. She loved sharing what she learned with others so they could benefit from her knowledge. Joelle was happiest when her tutoring helped improve the confidence and grades of a student.

Universities and Colleges sent correspondence and representatives asking her to consider enrolling. Joelle chose the best match for her goals and accelerated through the curriculums. She acquired two Bachelors Degrees, one in Math and the other in Education. Joelle received her teaching certificate and Masters in Education at twenty-two, then applied and was accepted into a doctoral program. She was offered numerous teaching opportunities by Ivy-League schools and other highly ranked universities. Joelle turned them all down. She took another path instead and followed her heart. She accepted a position teaching at a small private school for children in her home town of Philadelphia. She accepted the meager salary the school offered with the caveat she could design curriculum and use it to complete her doctorate. Joelle made sure the school added it in her contract.

Well Positioned

Ellison Construction, with Chay's leadership and Paul's partnership, expanded from home repairs to purchasing abandoned and dilapidated houses. Ellison Construction renovated and transformed the ugly eyesores into new beautiful living spaces improving the appearance of the communities and increasing property values. It was a profitable business because the city was experiencing a growth explosion and affordable housing was in high demand. Ellison Construction was able to sell the new homes at a fair price and still make a profit on their investments. The profits were divided between the six brothers.

Ellison Construction was well positioned. Chay had a plan to expand further into commercial development if they could raise the capital.

Chay saved a year's worth of unemployment pay courtesy of the USMC. Paul spent all his unemployment pay, but with their combined G. I. Bill loans there was enough to finance the expansion plan. Chay received full support from his brothers.

Meanwhile Joseph, now a resident at the local hospital, encouraged Chay to get a business degree. Chay

\

enrolled in Community College but he did not like the rules, the roster or the daily routine requiring extra classes he did not need; it felt like a waste of his time. He had enough of rules and routines in the military. He wanted to study the things that interested him. He preferred setting his own schedule, working with his hands and being on his feet instead of sitting on his rear listening to boring lectures. He liked to read but he was easily distracted so he dropped out of college and started his own self-study program by visiting the free library regularly. Chay had fond memories of being with his mother in the library. It became the perfect environment to further his education. Chay's intention was to learn how to expand the Ellison business. Fate decided he would expand the Ellison family.

First Impressions

Joelle caught a man watching her in the library. She had never seen him on her weekly visits, she would have noticed; he was not hard to miss. He towered over the children's bookshelves. He stopped looking at her but moved closer while he pulled books from the shelf. Joelle knew it was all a ruse, she doubted if he was seriously interested in medieval nursery rhymes. When he realized she was not fooled by his act he smiled. She liked his face, he had a deep dimple in his chin. She thought he was quite handsome. Joelle returned his smile then continued the reading lesson with her students.

Chay took the book on city zoning and building codes to a seat and started to read the introduction but his mind was on the teacher. He wandered around the library purposely killing time hoping to meet her. He retuned to the children's section just in time to see her give the last student a hug. The little boy looked very sad to say goodbye. He heard the boy call her, *'Miss Joelle'* before he left the library. When she was alone, Chay made his introduction. He spoke softly in the quiet of the library.

"Hello, my name is Charles, but most people call

me Chay."

Joelle was glad the man retuned. Her smile was friendly. She whispered, "Hello, Charles."

Charles asked, "Miss Joelle, is *Joelle* your first name?"

"Yes, it's easier for my students. My last name can be hard for some to pronounce." She pointed down to a notebook on the table. Charles leaned down to read the lettering. *'Joelle D. Duemijon'* was written in neat black cursive letters. He thought the penmanship was elegant. He assumed it was her handwriting.

"It's okay if you laugh. I'm used to it," she said as she slipped the notebook into her backpack with her library books and other belongings.

Charles had no idea what Joelle meant until he said her full name out loud slowly. "Jo-el...D....Doo-mee-jon. Oh...Oh...Ohhh!" After he heard how it sounded out loud, he could not control his laughter. He laughed so loud it echoed throughout the library and people turned in his direction. Joelle laughed too because his laughter was infectious, then she covered her mouth to muffle the sound. Charles was sorry when she smothered her laughter and covered her mouth. He thought she had a nice laugh and a nice mouth too. He could not help his thoughts or feelings, he thought she was a beautiful woman. Charles was smitten.

He lowered his voice back to a whisper, his tone was sympathetic but he was still smiling. "I can see why you were teased but I wish I was *John*," he admitted.

Joelle corrected him. She whispered, "It's pronounced ...*Doo/ay/may/jon*."

Charles whispered, "Du-ay-may-jon still sounds like I wish I was John."

Joelle blushed and turned her face away. Charles thought maybe he went too far so he changed the subject. "I noticed your students like to read Miss Joelle."

Joelle explained. "They're all brilliant, creative, talented children. We visit the library every Wednesday. I feel like they are my babies."

"You're very good with them. You look like you could be their mother." Charles tried to retract his statement. "I meant to say you look like you would make a good mother." His words did not come out the way he intended. He was embarrassed by his inept attempt to express his thoughts. He did not know it was the nicest compliment he could have given Joelle.

Joelle touched his arm in appreciation and to reassure him she was not offended. "Thank you for the compliment Charles," she said then she removed her hand from his arm and asked, "Do you have a last name?"

Charles answered, "Ellison and one day I hope you'll add it to yours." Charles could not believe he spoke his thoughts to a woman he just met. He was embarrassed again. He almost dropped the heavy book he forgot he was holding. His reflexes were sharp, he caught it before it hit the floor.

Joelle saw the book title and out of curiosity she asked, "Are you a construction worker?"

Charles was happy he had not chased her away. They walked to the library check out counter and he continued the conversation. "I have a business partnership with my brothers. We renovate old houses and rent or resell them. We're expanding." He pointed to the book. "This is going to help our business."

Joelle commented, "Sounds like you and your brothers will do well. Creating a company is a great goal to shoot for and a construction company is a good business."

Charles spoke confidently and with passion in his voice although he was still careful to keep his voice low. "Joelle it's not a goal. It's fact. My family has been in the construction business for years; my father started it and we're going to become one of the largest construction companies in this city and other cities too. We're going to employ more people, a lot more people in the future... and it's going to be a profitable business for the next generation...and...well...for a long time!"

Joelle whispered, "I see." She looked up at his face while he checked out his library book. She concluded he was probably much older than he looked. He was self-confident and her instincts told her whatever Charles, *most people call me Chay,* said he was going to do was going to get done. Joelle tugged the straps of her backpack over her shoulders securely and extended her hand. She said, "It was nice to meet you Charles Ellison. Perhaps I'll see you again next Wednesday."

Charles accepted Joelle's handshake but did not let go of her hand, he wished he was one of her students so he could get a hug. He seized the opportunity to get to know her better.

"Joelle, I would like to take you on a tour of some of our properties. You'll see how we create affordable housing. Are you available for a tour? Are you available?" Charles asked with his best 'playa' smile.

Joelle made direct eye contact and his 'playa' smile dissolved. Joelle's almond shaped chestnut brown eyes mesmerized Charles. Looking into Joelle's eyes made him feel like they were the only two people in the world. Charles could see why the boy was sad to leave Miss Joelle. He held his breath as he waited for her answer.

Joelle answered. "Yes and Yes."

Second Thoughts

Joelle thought Charles seemed like a nice man. He was a giant but his manner was gentle and unassuming. His palm was rough when they exchanged a handshake. His skin was smooth and dark. He looked as if he spent a great deal of time in the sun. Joelle wondered if his entire body was covered with the same dark chocolate that covered his bulging arm muscles.

Joelle remembered his presence, it was palpable when he stood beside her. There was a positive energy current flowing between them, it felt electric. He was flirtatious but respectable and she was entertained by his sense of humor. His eyes were kind they made her feel comforted and secure and she was enchanted by his charming face with his dimpled chin. She wondered if his father or mother had the same dimple. The facial feature was certainly a Mendelian inheritance. Joelle calculated the statistics and concluded at least one out of four of his children would inherit his cleft. It was a pleasant thought. She thought about his height being inherited too, but after she realized she was adding her own genetics into the equation, she redirected her thoughts. She just met the man and yet she was not surprised she was already thinking about a future with him.

The chemistry between them was undeniable but Joelle felt they shared more in common than just physical attraction. Their discussion about his business told her he was a man of action and loved his profession. Joelle was inspired by his devotion to his family and his affection for children. She thought it was complementary to her own feelings. Meeting Charles in a library was also a good sign. Charles seemed to be a mature, resourceful and ambitious man. She estimated he was at least five years older than her but it was only a guess. She was not going to try to calculate it, she would ask him how old he was the next time she saw him. She thought he was definitely someone worth her time. She wanted get to know him better. Joelle did not know Charles Randolph Ellison Jr. would change her life.

Charles noticed everything about Joelle in the short time he spent with her at the library. She was young but she was definitely a mature woman. Her hands were small and delicate yet she shook his hand with a firm grip. Her nails were natural and well manicured. He was especially happy about her unadorned left hand ring finger. He remembered the way she covered her mouth with her pretty hands to smother her laughter; her laugh was memorable. He also remembered when she touched his arm during their conversation; he thought it was a good sign.

He thought Duemijon was an interesting name. He did not know its origin but he could tell Joelle's momma or daddy was black because her features were definitely from the motherland. He was struck by her natural beauty but it was more than Joelle's physical appearance that pulled him in her direction. He was attracted by the radiance of her inner beauty. Light shined through her smiles, a light that warmed him when he stood next to her. He wanted to add things to her light to make it burn brighter so he could continue to be near her glow and feel the warmth. He wanted Joelle D. Duemijon to be a part of his life and by the time he left the library he was determined to make it happen. Charles knew he met the love of his life.

Perspectives

The Ellison Brothers were worried Chay would not be able to maintain his level of involvement with the business. They thought with a new young girlfriend their brother would be on lock-down and unavailable. There was no need to worry because Chay actually gained momentum when Joelle entered his life. The Ellison Brothers were surprised Chay met a beauty with brains. Joelle was the smartest person they ever encountered. She had her own interest and career but she proved to be a great partner for Chay. Joelle was positive, encouraging and a staunch supporter of the Ellison construction business.

Joelle blended in easily with the Ellison family and she earned the respect of the brothers. Joelle shared common interests with Joseph concerning his work with the HBCUs and the hospital. She bonded with Ronald over calculations and financial balance sheets. She held deep conversations with Byron about human behaviors. Gene was in awe of Joelle because she could also play musical instruments. He said she played piano so well she could join his band anytime.

The Ellison Brothers were happy when Chay

asked to marry Joelle but they teased him and said he was too old for her and she was only marrying him for his money. Charles took it all in stride. He was still shocked Joelle agreed to marry him. He kept thinking one day she was going to tell him he was just a part of a learning experiment. Deep down in his heart, he knew Joelle truly loved him because she showed it every day.

Joelle liked her brother-in-laws and she thought highly of the special relationships they shared. She observed the love, devotion and respect they had for each other. They were a tight bunch of siblings. She sensed each brother would protect the other to the death if necessary. Joelle found it admirable. She saw the same qualities in her new brothers in her new husband. The Ellison Brothers shared an unbreakable family bond and a common drive to succeed; yet even with the same physical traits, each brother was uniquely different. Joelle found the Ellison Brothers were a fascinating group of men.

In the beginning of Joelle's relationship with Charles she had reservations about Paul. Charles and Paul were extremely close. Paul was dedicated to Charles and Joelle had concerns about his dependency on him. She thought Paul might compete with her for his brother's attention, but Paul gave them space and was still available whenever Charles needed him. Joelle thought Paul just wanted to please his older brother.

Joelle had a discussion with Charles about her feelings concerning Paul. Charles assured her Paul was just looking out for the family's best interests. He told her Paul tried to please everyone as a way of making up for what he thought were his shortcomings. Charles confessed he admired Paul the most out of his five brothers. He explained to Joelle, "Paul deals with the world on his own terms and that's exhausting for a Black Man in America." He took Joelle's hand as he spoke. "If I'd gone through everything Paul has dealt with …from the core, during the war, after the war and now fighting a new war with his mental and physical afflictions, I don't think I would have survived. Paul has the strength and perseverance few men possess; he's the bravest man I have ever known…with the exception of my father. I have you in my life Jo, Paul has no one in his life except his brothers."

Joelle's perspective changed when she saw Paul through her husband's eyes.

Developments

Dr. Joelle Duemijon's educational curriculum for children received national recognition and many awards. Her work was published and private schools wanted to hire her services to use her program for its proven success. The Philadelphia School for the Gifted offered Dr. Joelle Duemijon a Director position and she accepted.

Charles secured the first ECC commercial building contract and said they were doing well financially. Charles laughed and raised his eyebrows mischievously. "Thanks to Ron, the finance man, we can afford twins."

They decided after they were married for one year to stop practicing birth control and let nature take its course. Charles was ten years older than Joelle and he was eager to start their family. He hoped for good news every month. Joelle encouraged Charles to work at it more frequently. Charles was happy to oblige.

Joelle was a spontaneous and creative lover. One evening she arranged for them to meet to celebrate their accomplishments. Charles waited in the back office of the building he shared with Joseph. Joelle arrived dressed in canvas construction overalls, work boots and not another stitch of clothing. It was a love session to go down in their record book. Charles said he was glad they were able to squeeze the session in before her menstrual cycle. Joelle confessed she suspected she was already pregnant. Charles insisted they make love again for extra measure.

Joelle's pregnancy was a welcomed gift and with only a month to go Charles knew it was a boy, although he really did not care as long as the baby was healthy and Joelle pulled through. He heard some awful stories about labor and childbirth. He went back to the library and checked out as many books as he could on the subject. Charles studied the facts so he could follow his wife's progress. He learned about the forty weeks of gestation and trimesters. He learned about the stages of his baby's development in his woman's womb. He also learned how Joelle's body was changing and the impacts on her emotional state. He was particularly interested in how to help Joelle have an easier labor. He made it to all the birthing classes and learned how to coach her breathing. He hoped he would not be too emotional when the time came.

Charles was excited and scared at the same time. He read books on fatherhood responsibilities too. Joelle told him the books were all theoretical and each pregnancy was unique. She reassured him he would be a good father. She promised he would get plenty of on the job training.

Under Construction

Joelle stroked the soft delicate crocheted material of a little yellow bonnet then placed it in the baby's dresser drawer. A group of Joelle's friends, colleagues and some parents of her students surprised her with a baby shower at the school. Charles was in on the whole secret.

Joelle was cracking up with laughter while her big, burly, strong as the Hulk, husband struggled up the stairs with pastel colored balloons, boxes and shopping bags. He put the gifts around the room in a colorful array and tied the balloons to the crib; then he helped Joelle settle down comfortably in one of the two oversized rocking chairs. He sat in the other chair and continued to share more of his plans.

It was a critical time for the city construction business. The bid process was in progress and moving at a rapid pace. City contracts were a prosperous investment and the Ellison Brothers wanted in. They all contributed to the site proposal. Ellison Construction planned to build new offices at the site. Charles would present it to the city officials. There was a lot riding on the next move and they were depending on Charles.

"We still need to finalize the development plans

but the proposal is sound and I secured the permits early. I'm going to present in front of the city planning commission, city council and bunch of business associations...and...well...there's more to do after that... but I know we're in. I'll meet up with the guys as soon as I get the official go from the city."

Joelle loved her husband's confidence. She told Charles, "Babe, I'm really excited for you and your brothers."

Charles stood up to walk around the baby's nursery he built in their new home. He looked at his wife. Joelle was relaxed in the rocker ready to listen to more details. Charles forgot about everything when he looked at Joelle. He thought she was more beautiful than the first day they met in the library. Joelle was radiant she looked joyful. Charles beamed with pride at his pregnant wife. She was going to make him a father. Their first child, his son was going to carry on the Ellison name and the Ellison business.

Joelle rose slowly from the rocking chair. Charles watched anxiously and when he saw her wince after she kicked her shoes off he asked, "Babe you okay?" Joelle moved over to her husband. She rubbed her round bulging belly. She was in her third trimester, the eighth month. "My feet are swelling but I feel fantastic. Our *girl* is very active today," she said. Charles grinned and played along."Really, well it was a big day for our *boy, he's* excited to see all *his* gifts?"

Charles saw their baby moving and pressing against the smooth brown caramel skin of Joelle's tummy. Charles massaged her stomach and the baby kicked. Charles jumped and Joelle laughed at his surprised reaction.

"I told you. *She's* been doing that all day, *she* knows we had a party."

Charles told her, "*He's* showing *he's* ready to get to work."

Joelle giggled and Charles gave her a long passionate kiss. He found her tongue and toyed with it playfully with his own knowing how it would affect her. She accepted his kiss while enjoying the familiar texture, taste and pleasure of his lips and mouth. They parted lips but Charles did not let her go.

Joelle teased, "You do know it's too late to make twins right?" Charles laughed and planted soft kisses on her neck. Joelle caressed his face and asked, "How are *you* feeling?" Charles turned her around and encircled her in his arms from behind. She gained weight with the pregnancy and he liked the extra junk in her trunk. He pulled her close to whisper in her ear. "I always feel good when I'm with you My Love."

Joelle closed her eyes and leaned back into his hard body. Charles was her gentle giant. She was in love with him and she knew Charles loved her in return. She thought it was destiny they found each other without looking. She was thrilled to be carrying his child.

"We need to think of names." Joelle said while enjoying his closeness. Charles anticipated the subject. "I've been thinking of naming him Alexander. It was my Mom's maiden name, but it can be used for a boy's first name, right?"

Charles leaned down to nestle his chin into his wife's soft shoulder. Joelle craned her neck around and he bent over to make full contact with her lips again. He kissed her until she broke the kiss off with a moan. Charles was pleased knowing he created the desire in his woman he intended.

Joelle took a moment to compose herself before she spoke. "We're in the same book, but I went back a chapter." She laughed and offered her suggestion. "We could name *her* Harper after *her* great-grandmother Beulah Harper-Ellison and it would honor George Harper too. Our baby would have both your family names."

Charles thought the suggestion was brilliant. "Harper is a good name for a *boy* too," he said and gave Joelle a gentle squeeze. He began to grind against her plump bottom while he rocked her in his arms. He placed soft kisses on her neck and positioned himself so she could feel his arousal.

Joelle rubbed her belly and spoke to their baby, "Harper, your Daddy is trying to make you a brother or sister before you get here."

Charles rubbed his erection against Joelle's backside. He lifted up her dress and pulled down her panties. He whispered, "According to my research, we can have just as much sex as before as long as you're comfortable. Are you comfortable?"

"Umm-hmmm," Joelle said while enjoying the feeling of her husband's hands pressed against her. Charles asked. "Want me to stop?" Joelle could hear his desire in the tone of his voice. She did not want Charles to stop, she wanted the pleasure he could give. She leaned against his body to encourage him.

Charles made love to Joelle entering her gently from behind, carefully holding her close to him, easily lifting her despite her extra body weight. He eased himself in and out of his wife while lifting her up and down to his rhythm. He began to pleasure her the way she preferred. When he felt she was ready to climax he held back so he could fully experience her body's reaction and the orgasmic tightening convulsions from her vagina. It was exquisite. He could no longer contain himself; he exploded all his love inside of her sweating against her back with her dress up between them and his shirt plastered to his chest from his exertion. He picked her up and carried her effortlessly to the master bedroom, then laid her down on their bed. He removed her dress and exposed her plump swollen breast, her nipples were erect and firm preparing to nurse their child, her tummy was fully extended making her small belly-button poke out. He stroked her face, breast, stomach and thighs. Joelle was under his spell. He kissed her lips and her swollen breast before he helped her into her lounging robe. Once she was settled back in bed he put his ear to her belly to hear his child's heartbeat. Joelle kissed the top of his head affectionately and fell asleep.

Charles listened to his wife's soft breathing and the steady thump-thump of his child's rapid heart beat. His wife slept soundly while his child was at play. He was astounded when Joelle's stomach jumped and shifted as their baby kicked and stretched in her womb. Joelle stirred from her slumber when she felt the baby moving but she kept her eyes closed. She mumbled, "Come on Babe, please leave Harper alone so we can rest." Charles reluctantly complied with her request. "Okay Harper, Mommy's tired so we're going to let her sleep." He kissed Joelle's belly then he kissed her cheek and whispered, "Get some rest My Love."

Proposal #4515

Charles was denied entrance into the room and told the city meeting was cancelled. He did not believe it so he asked the official city clerk for more information. The clerk was arrogant and seemed in a hurry to brush him off when he asked for the proposal number and company name. He checked a log book, shook his head and looked up at Charles but spoke to him as if he were a child.

"The bid process is on a cycle. The cycle was extended and the Ellison Construction isn't listed on the log."

The clerk tried to go back inside the meeting room. Charles blocked the door and the clerk was clearly annoyed. Charles moved in closer. He stood over the little white man knowing he was intimidated by his size and race. Charles used it to his advantage and told him to explain. The clerk's voice was shaky when he spoke again. "Proposal number 4515 submitted by Ellison Construction was disqualified. The permits expired and no new applications or request for extensions were submitted." The clerk explained further, "Ellison Construction did not acquire the proper permits. The permits previously granted were not in effect, therefore proposal 4515 and all bids submitted with said proposal were nullified."

To add insult to injury, Charles was told, a new qualified proposal was submitted and accepted so another construction company secured the land. The Ellison Construction Company would receive a cease and desist order and was restricted by law from all access to the site.

The clerk was satisfied with his own explanation so he gave Charles a sheet of paper with a list of dates for the next bid cycle. Charles stepped aside and the clerk stepped around him carefully then entered the meeting room and closed the door. Charles thought he heard him lock it.

Charles was devastated. His brothers were expecting to celebrate, instead he would be delivering bad news. How was he going to explain his mistake? How had the bid and proposal been accepted, then disqualified and undercut? Charles was sure they were a lock-in, he was confident ECC submitted the lowest bid. Charles was told the city meeting was just a formality to close out the process. This was a complete reversal of fortune. He never heard about a change in the bidding cycle, he never thought about the city changing the rules. It was a risk he never considered. He was busy preparing to present to the city council. Charles figured in his eagerness to file sixty days before they acquired the rights to the site the permits expired and were no longer valid because of the delay in the bid process. It was a catch twenty-two; without the proper permits, even if the original proposal was accepted, the bid would be disqualified.

Charles drove back to the small backroom office and called the only person that could lift his heavy heart.

Framework

Joelle answered on the first ring. "Hey Babe," she said followed by a long drawn-out yawn.

Charles asked, "How are you My Love?" Joelle told him, "I'm good, just woke up from a nap, can't believe I slept so long." Charles was thankful everything was fine at home. The baby was due in two weeks. Joelle was sleeping a lot. He enjoyed watching her sleep or catching her drifting off in the nursery on the window seat while she was supposed to be reading. She was the center of his calm. He closed his eyes and imagined Joelle at home wishing he was with her. He admitted, "I needed to hear your voice."

Joelle pulled her robe around her bulging belly and swung her swollen feet around to the floor. She was resting in bed but the tone in her husband's voice was disturbing. "Charles, please tell me what's wrong, what happened?"

Charles regretted he was telling Joelle the news over the phone. He did not want to take any chances with her delicate condition. "I'm sorry, I shouldn't be worrying you about this right now. It can wait til I get home."

He listened as her soothing voice addressed his hesitancy.

"Charles, I'm okay, the baby is okay. We're both healthy. I'm not going to break. Harper is feeling just as strong as her Big Daddy. You called because you must need to talk, so talk to me. You can tell me anything. What's going on?"

Joelle always knew exactly what to say; it was just one of the many reasons Charles loved her. Joelle reminded him she was capable of handling whatever came her way and Charles knew she was right. Joelle was a strong woman.

"I love you Warrior Queen, you are my strength," he said truthfully.

Charles breathed a long sigh. Everything was better when he talked it out with his woman. Joelle always gave him hope. He took a deep breath and poured his heart out over the phone.

"We lost the bid. I didn't have a chance to present, some clerk told me the land was sold to another company. I have no idea how far this will set us back. Jo, I've got to tell the guys I jumped the gun with the permits."

Charles could not say anything else without a

choking sound in his voice so he waited for Joelle to say something. There was a brief silence. Charles pressed the phone closer to his ear until he heard Joelle speak his thoughts.

"You think it's your fault and you let your brothers down. Your brothers look to you to help guide them. You feel like you failed them."

Joelle continued speaking while she put on her slippers and headed toward the bathroom with the cordless phone. The pressure on her bladder was painful after her long nap. She made it just in time, she kept talking as she relieved herself.

"You think it might be hard for them to trust your leadership in the future and you wouldn't blame them because you would probably feel the same way if you were in their shoes."

Joelle held the phone in one hand while she cleaned herself and pushed herself up from the commode. She tucked the phone in between her shoulder and chin to wash her hands. It was difficult because her big belly was taking up the space between the sink and the faucet.

Charles found his voice again, he told her, "Please

continue… you're saying it a lot better than I can."

Joelle sat down on the padded bench in the master bathroom and leaned back into a more comfortable position. She pictured Charles sitting in his office feeling disappointed.

"Charles, I love you, your brothers love you, your baby is going to love you. It's that simple. Things happen in life and in business. It's how we react as a result of what happens that really matters."

Charles thought his wife was not only intelligent she was wise. Joelle was the voice of reason. Her counsel changed his negative thoughts. He spoke to her lovingly. "In other words, Mrs. Ellison, the question is *What am I going to do about it?*"

"Correct Mr. Ellison, you get an A plus!" Joelle laughed then screamed and dropped the phone.

Early Arrival

Charles hung up the phone on Joelle so he could dial 911. He was calm when he provided his home address and the nature of the emergency, then he rushed out of the office and headed straight to the hospital.

He could not get the sound of Joelle's scream out of his head. He did not know her condition or what happened. He was worried and scared for Joelle and their baby. He also felt guilty for telling Joelle bad news over the phone.

Charles blew through every red light until he reached the hospital. He was distraught and infuriated after he was informed he arrived ahead of the ambulance.

Expectations

The intense pain Joelle experienced made her scream out and drop the phone. It was like a sharp spear was driven into her lower back. She tried to get up from the bench but the pain was so acute she screamed again. Her scream was cut off when all her muscles suddenly seized and locked up into a spasm. She tried to move but she could not. She tried to speak but her mouth was frozen. She was paralyzed. This was not the labor pain she expected, something was wrong. The elegant monogramed 'CE & JE' towels slipped off the towel bar as she fell off the bench and hit the stone tiled floor. The impact was a jarring blow against her abdomen; it knocked the wind out of her too. She focused on the tiles until she was able to catch her breath; and when her breath returned she prayed for her baby with her face pressed against the bathroom floor.

Joelle recovered from the temporary paralysis and as her muscles relaxed she rolled onto her back to relieve the pressure off her stomach. She caressed her belly and prayed her baby was unharmed. She was able to pull herself up and walk back to the bedroom to get the bag she prepared for the birth. She stepped slowly down the stairs being careful to hold onto the bannister. She heard the sirens before she saw the flashing lights outside the stained glassed windows of the front door. Then another spasm hit and it felt like a giant egg cracked between her legs. She stood with her legs apart as water gushed from her womb onto the black and white harlequin patterned marble floor Charles meticulously set and polished.

Connections

The emergency call came from Mr. Charles Ellison. He reported his wife, Joelle, was pregnant and something was wrong. She was alone at their residence and she needed immediate help.

The ambulance raced through the city streets with the siren blaring and lights flashing. Two experienced emergency medical technicians, Dan Shepherd and Scott Hurd were in route. There was an unspoken communication between the two men as Scott maneuvered the ambulance through traffic with precision and urgency.

Dr. Joelle Ellison was admired and respected by everyone in the hospital. She designed a learning program for the pediatrics department. She convinced the hospital board, including her brother-in-law Joseph, to fund a new library for the children in order to implement the program. The project was approved when ECC volunteered to provide the labor and construction.

The ManDane Children's Library was always filled with children and families who visited the hospital. They enjoyed speaking with the teachers or reading from hundreds of donated books from the colorful bookshelves. Children with chronic illnesses confined to the hospital for longer terms had access to tutors to continue learning during their stay. Dr. Joelle was also a volunteer tutor.

Dan Shepherd's eight-year old son, Little Danny, was often a benefactor of the tutoring. Dan met Dr. Joelle on one of his frequent visits to the hospital library with his son. Dr. Joelle was well liked by the children, she shook Dan's hand and hugged Little Danny. Dan thanked the doctor for all she had contributed to the hospital. Dan was surprised and humbled when the doctor thanked him too. She was sincere when she explained to him EMTs were heroes for all the people they helped in the community. She reminded him he was essential to saving lives. Dan Shepherd remembered Dr. Joelle's words and kindness. He hoped the call was routine.

Transport

Joelle recognized Dan when she opened the door. He rushed to her side while she gave him instructions. "Dan, I fell in the bathroom, get a stretcher please. I don't think I can walk and my water just broke," she said.

Dan left briefly then returned with Scott, a stretcher, sheets, blankets and towels. Joelle tried to remain calm as she experienced a new painful contraction. It was concentrated in the small of her back. The searing pain intensified. She rode the wave until it slowly dissipated. She wondered if her pain was normal. She cried out to Dan as she reached for his hand and squeezed. "Please hurry!" She rubbed her rigid tummy while she spoke to her baby. "Hold on Harper." Then she cried out again when another painful contraction hit. "Oh God, why does it hurt so much? Please hurry!"

Dan and Scott were fast, efficient and careful. They secured Joelle to the stretcher, grabbed the bag with her personal belongings and placed her inside the ambulance smoothly. Dan climbed up into the back of the ambulance still holding Joelle's hand. He sat on a bench bolted into the truck. His reassuring voice floated above her head. "Dr. Joelle, everything is going to be fine.

Try not to push, breathe through each contraction."

Joelle let go of Dan's hand so he could do his job. He placed a monitor around her stomach and another on her index finger. She squeezed her eyes shut and counted to gauge the timing of her labor. Scott closed the ambulance doors and jumped in behind the wheel. Dan repeated, "Everything is going to be fine." Joelle prayed Dan was right.

Harper Demi Ellison

Charles leaned over the hospital bed in the delivery room holding Joelle's hand, coaching her, massaging her lower back between contractions. Joelle refused the epidural drugs, she was not taking any chances. Charles was unaware Joelle was afraid of experiencing the paralysis she suffered earlier. Charles allowed her to squeeze his hand until his fingers went numb. He gave her his other hand while the numb hand regained circulation. He fed her crushed ice and placed cool towels on her forehead. He kept her focused on her breathing during the four hours of labor. He never left her side. He watched her sweat, grunt, scream and pant. He cried as he watched his woman work through the pain and struggle to bring life into the world.

Charles witnessed a miracle.

Harper Demi Ellison weighed in at six pounds, three ounces and measured nineteen inches long. The moment Charles laid eyes on his new born child he forgot about having a son. He fell in love with his baby girl. She was healthy and she was beautiful. She had a full head of slick dark hair but a few curls were sticking up on top of her head like a little crown. Charles was surprised Harper was so pink until he remembered what his mother said when Gene was born. *"Sometime Black babies are born pink until the African genes kick in, then they brown up. You can usually tell how brown they're going to get by looking at the tips of the ears or the pigment around the cuticles."* At the time Charles paid his mother no mind, she was always saying something that went over his head as a child; as he grew older her words always seemed to come back to his mind in the right circumstances.

Charles inspected his new baby girl's ears. They were tiny and perfectly shaped and the delicate tips were a light cocoa brown. Her eyes were open but they were hidden by wispy featherlike eyelashes. Harper's cherub face looked like Joelle's. Her fingers and plump little hands were balled into miniature fists. Charles could only see her thumb but the cuticle was brown.

The proud grandparents, Manuela and Dane Duemijon, arrived at the hospital. They doted over their first grandchild. Harper's uncles welcomed her arrival too. They broke the rules and crowded the private hospital room so each could get a chance to see Harper up close. Paul held her last and for the longest time. Joelle watched Paul's interaction with her daughter. Joelle saw her husband's reflection in Paul's expression. Paul grinned at

Harper while he tenderly cradled her in his strong arms.

"She's beautiful Jo," Paul said as he handed Harper back over to Joelle. He gave Charles a pat on his back. "You did good Bro, congratulations."

Everyone was caught up in the excitement of the birth. Harper was the first Ellison of the next generation. They said she was the greatest gift Joelle could have given to the family. Charles and Joelle were proud parents simply because they created a healthy child not because of the significance of continuing the Ellison bloodline. Charles and Joelle believed Harper was a gift from God that showed the world their love was real.

Next Location

Joelle's stay at the hospital gave Charles time to think up a new plan. He pulled Paul out of the room during the family visit. He told Paul everything including his suspicions the city was playing foul. Paul thought it was best to postpone telling their brothers until they had more details.

Paul gave Charles a fist bump. "Don't worry Bro, family comes first, you can pick up business after Jo and Harper come home."

Charles agreed, "Okay but we need a new plan. Can you scout out new locations while I handle things here?" Paul's expression told Charles he did not need to ask.

"I'm on it. Go back in there and tell Jo I said congrats again. Imma slide on outta here."

Charles and Paul exchanged their customary handshake in the hospital hallway then Paul left to get to work.

Paul developed a substantial list of properties, it included stores with attached apartments and abandoned businesses within the low-income residential areas. Some of the property locations were listed as 'risky' neighborhoods and were readily available for purchase. Charles and Paul settled on two locations they agreed looked promising.

One location was in a rezoned residential district. Most of the houses were abandoned eyesores in a neighborhood riddled with colorful graffiti, overgrown weeds and trash. Paul said he used to meet people in the back of the old houses. Charles had a good idea what kind of people Paul met and the reason for his meetings but he made no comment. Paul reminded Charles they renovated a large foster home in the area. He met the community leaders and the kids from the home. He liked the community. Paul pointed out the connected properties gave ECC residential and commercial investments. He reasoned the area was an untapped potential for economic growth in the city. Paul was enthusiastic about the find. It was his preferred choice.

The second location was an old steel factory on the river front. It included a warehouse with boat slips. The factory had fallen into ruin after outsourcing forced its closure, but the warehouse and slips were in good condition. There was an enormous space for secured storage; large enough for heavy construction equipment, tools and supplies. The pier access provided ECC the opportunity to ship materials and sail in and across the Delaware River. Paul was sure the factory would still clear an engineering inspection.

Paul said, "Bro, the price is a steal, no pun intended."

Charles thanked Paul for his thorough research. He told him he thought the pier location was the better option.

Best Choice

Joelle prepared for the baby to nurse. Harper snuggled up against her breast comfortably tucked in her arms; her tiny hand curled around Joelle's pinky-finger. She turned her head and latched on. Her little chubby cheeks contracted and expanded as she sucked. Her almond shaped eyes were identical to her mother's, they were wide open and focused on Joelle's face. Charles sat in a reclining chair close to the hospital bed watching the bond build between mother and child. Harper's calm temperament was a mirrored reflection of Joelle's. He was waiting for the nurse to return with a copy of the hospital discharge papers so he could take his family home.

Joelle and Charles spoke in soft whispers in the sanctity of the quiet room. Joelle looked down at Harper as she spoke to Charles. "Paul's location sounds like the best choice to me. It's a wonderful idea to showcase the exceptional work of ECC. It takes skill and vision to take old buildings, renovate them, restore them back to life and raise a community to a new level. It would revitalize the neighborhood and give the people hope. It would improve the property values, not to mention provide good press for the business. Paul's choice is the best

Charles." Joelle asked Harper, "What do you think little-one?"

Charles squeezed onto the edge of the narrow hospital bed. Joelle scooted over and adjusted her dress so he did not sit on it. He planted his foot firmly on the floor for support and managed to get close enough to place his arm around Joelle's shoulders without disrupting the feeding. He looked down into his little girl's eyes and whispered, "Harper, should Daddy open up his office in the hood?"

Harper turned her head away from her feeding when she heard her father's voice. She let out a loud burp. Charles laughed and said, "Harper Demi Ellison and Joelle Duemijon-Ellison, I love you both so much. I'm a happy man."

Charles started to get up to fetch the car. Joelle pulled him back before he could get away. She touched the dimple in his chin and gave him a long kiss. It took his breath away. "We love you too. We'll be waiting right here Big Daddy." She picked up Harper's tiny hand and waved. Charles grinned like he won the lottery.

New Hope

Charles left his Queen and Princess to fetch the chariot. He left the oversized truck at home and installed Harper's new infant car seat in the back seat of Joelle's practical and more efficient car. There were twelve long-stemmed red roses wrapped in a box for Joelle and a small bouquet of wildflowers waiting in the car for Harper.

His thoughts turned to protecting his daughter's future. Charles believed Paul and Joelle were right; making bold and unexpected moves would raise Ellison Construction to another level. They could make it work using their own means and on their own terms. The new plan reminded Charles of what his father taught them about the obligation to fulfill their roles as leaders in their community. ECC would live up to Pop Ellison's legacy. ECC would lead by creating, building, restoring and employing in the Black community.

Charles could hardly contain his excitement when he paid the parking attendant. He was a father! Harper gave him more motivation. Charles drove his family home with renewed confidence and new hope.

Home Coming

There was are private family barbecue to celebrate Harper's birth. Charles made his famous ribs and chicken on the grill with home grown roasted vegetables and sweet watermelon for the gathering. Charles turned into a great cook. The sunroom was filled with deep baritone voices punctuated occasionally with Joelle's soft laughter. Charles set the meal on the table while his brothers spent time fawning and cooing over his daughter. He was grateful for the love and support his brothers gave Joelle.

"Harper is beautiful. Thank God she looks like Joelle!" Gene said jokingly as he took a seat at the table.

"Thanks Bro." Charles took no offense because he agreed.

"Well done Lil Jo," Byron's said using the nickname he gave his sister-in-law to distinguish her from his brother. Byron was into his second helping, enjoying the food and the happy gathering.

Joelle eyes were focused on Harper's little face as she held her close. "Awwww, Thanks guys for the compliments but I think we both did well," she said.

Joseph tapped the side of his beer bottle and

cleared his throat before he spoke.

"Congratulations to Charles and Joelle! Welcome to the family Princess Harper! Cheers to a new generation of Ellisons!" Joseph turned to Charles and added, "You're going to be a great father Chay…You had a lot of practice with us."

Charles laughed and playfully shoved Joseph away.

Gene reminded everyone by stating the obvious, "Harper isn't one of the boys…she's a guuuurl!"

Charles grinned then groaned, "Man, I'm already thinking about building a moat around the house and filling it with alligators."

The Ellison Brothers nodded in agreement with Charles.

Paul confirmed. "We'll help you build it Bro!"

Charles looked serious. Joelle erupted in laughter first, then his brothers laughed too realizing the absurdity of their thinking.

Joelle stood and Charles was immediately by her side. He pulled the chair away from the table and assisted.

"I'm stuffed so now I'm taking Harper upstairs to the nursery so she can eat too." There was side-splitting laughter when Joelle proclaimed Harper inherited the Ellison appetite gene while Byron sucked on a barbecued rib bone.

Joseph reminded Joelle, "Keep taking the prenatal vitamins to keep your energy level up." Joelle was grateful for the extra care. "Thanks *Uncle Doctor Joe*," she teased then added, "We have a follow-up visit scheduled next week, but we're doing great." Joseph liked his new monicker.

Charles and Joelle allowed each of the uncles to get a last look at Harper. She was wide awake and unbothered by all the attention. Harper captured all of their hearts. The uncles reluctantly allowed her to retire.

Charles escorted Joelle and Harper upstairs to the nursery. He fluffed up the pillows in one of the rocking chairs and helped them settle in comfortably. He watched as Joelle exposed her breast and prepared to nurse. Harper squirmed around in Joelle's arms eagerly anticipating her feeding. Harper found her own small fist and placed it in her mouth and starting sucking it; when the results were not as she expected her eyes opened wide in surprise, she frowned and cried out. Charles and Joelle laughed at their child's animated expression.

Harper latched on hungrily. She made loud sucking sounds and her facial expression filled with contentment and satisfaction as she suckled the natural source of nourishment her mother provided. Joelle and Charles shared the intimate moment alone with their baby girl. Charles would have spent the rest of the evening watching his two favorite loves but his brothers were downstairs waiting. Joelle read his mind and whispered to him, "Go handle your business, we're good."

Charles knelt down and kissed Joelle softly. He touched Harper's tiny brow before he left to rejoin his brothers.

New Direction

Charles and Paul stood in the family room while everyone else found a comfortable place to sit. Byron relaxed on the sofa snacking and Gene sat next to him. Joseph and Ronald took seats in the double-wide chairs. Paul stood to the side and waited for Charles to start.

Charles started with the facts. "We didn't get the city contract. The bid period was extended and our permits expired. They said we needed new permits to submit the proposal so ECC was disqualified."

Ronald sensed something was afoot. He was outraged but he kept his voice down so he did not disturb Joelle and Harper upstairs. "You mean the city screwed us out of a profitable opportunity!"

Ronald was the Chief Financial Officer of Ellison Construction. He felt responsible for the proposal's financial components. He ran the numbers over in his head, he was sure they proposed a fair price. He was calculating the amount that might have edged them out.

He asked, "How much did it go for?"

Charles responded. "I don't know Ron. I'm going to leave it up to you to find out."

Ronald accepted the directive with a head nod.

Byron voiced his thoughts. "It all sounds fishy to me; first we're in and now we're out. Something's not right y'all."

Joseph was quiet.

Gene spoke, "Oh you mean something's white."

Ronald said with conviction. "I'll do some digging around and figure out what really happened."

Gene seconded Ron's idea, he raised his beer and took a sip. "Right-on!" Then Gene said sarcastically. "And what really happened to the notification about the extension? I guess it got lost in the mail."

There was an open discussion with varying opinions and suspicions of city wrong doing. Charles brought the meeting back to order. He told his brothers, "I know this is a disappointment and I'm sorry."

Charles was sincere. He looked into each of his brother's faces and what he saw moved him. His brothers were not disappointed with him nor were they wavering on his leadership abilities; on the contrary they were listening and ready to hear his next direction. His brothers trusted his leadership. Charles felt confident when he announced the next move.

"Proposal 4515 is dead...but it doesn't matter... because we have a new direction with new options. ECC is going to focus on a new vision, a new plan, a better plan; and once we execute it successfully the city will be begging for us to take on their projects." Charles looked at Paul with pride. "Tell them about your research Bro."

New Leader

Charles abdicated the floor to Paul. He took a seat between Byron and Gene on the couch, opened a cold beer and prepared to listen with his brothers.

Paul was a little caught off guard but he was quick on his feet, it served him well all his life. He stepped into the center of the room and started sharing his research. He gave detail information for both locations, including history, square footage, land survey data and zoning information. He committed it to memory but he had notes ready. Paul finished by telling his brothers he was excited about the location in the community and it was his first choice. "It's prime real estate and considering the expected revitalization, rezoning and expansion of the district, it's going to be the future for us... a foothold in the Black community. It takes us to the next level and it gives ECC office space in a proper building." Paul was referring to the medical office building Joseph owned. It was not a good fit for a construction company's office especially if they intended to expand.

Paul hesitated then looked at Ron. "The largest property has been abandoned for a while and there are leans, and taxes ... to clean up...but... I tracked down the property owner and it's nothing Ron can't manage based on what we were prepared to pay for the 4515 project downtown." Paul smiled at Ron showing the confidence he had in him then turned to address all his brothers. "The building is incredible, it still has the original architecture and much of it can be restored. There's a small piece of land around it too. I hired the kids from the foster home in the neighborhood to clean up the weeds and trash. It's got great potential for our expansion. I can take y'all to see it."

Charles admitted to Paul's surprise, "Paul's right, the community location has potential but if we're going to move, we better move fast."

Ronald's anger was abated after realizing the new plan turned a negative into a positive. "I agree with Paul's preference. It's the better location plus I think trying to pull something off on the Delaware pier might be a long-shot especially after we just loss the downtown project." Ron looked at Charles.

Charles tried not to show it, but he was hurt by Ron's reminder of the loss.

Paul defended Charles, "Ron we didn't lose the project, somebody stole it from under us."

Ron countered, "Paul I'm not saying the pier isn't a possibility. I'm saying it may be more complicated than the project we bid on in center city. Let me redo the numbers and if they add up maybe we can invest in both locations."

Joseph cautioned, "We don't want to bite off more than we can chew and I think Ron's point is valid. It's going to be tough trying to get Delgado to give up the pier."

Paul explained. "The factory and warehouse are privately owned and priced to sell. The owners don't have a choice. They're under some kind of time constraint to dump the property to help them file for bankruptcy before everything goes public and the shit hits the fan. Word on the street is the factory shut down because of mismanagement."

Ronald reacted to the new information with interest. "That changes the variables," he said.

Byron added his opinion, "I think we should develop offices in the community first." Byron asked the group, "What do y'all think?"

Gene stood up to announce his answer. "Y'all know the hood location is a good move. It's what Pops would have wanted. We can make this thing happen for the future of our people. Power to the People. Right On."

Ronald and Byron put fists up in the air.

Byron shouted, "Right-on for the next generation!" Then he looked up at the ceiling hoping his outburst did not disturb Joelle and Harper upstairs. All was quiet. Gene returned to his seat on the sofa.

Joseph spoke to Paul. "Gene's right, it's what Pops would have wanted us to do. I don't need to see it, if you say it's good, I'm good."

Paul sat on the piano bench with his back toward the numerous family photos Joelle restored and arranged on the piano top. He spoke honestly. "They're always going to put a foot on our neck and we're not going to get the opportunities the white construction companies will get in this city. We can't let them stop us though, we got to keep it moving. This decision requires everyone's agreement in order to proceed. It's risky. It will have long-term impacts on ECC business and it's a substantial investment of money, time, and material. ECC's reputation will be at stake on this one for sure, so we gotta do it right. It's also going to create more adversaries but like Pops always told us, *We are Stronger when United.*"

The room was so quiet they could hear Joelle moving around upstairs. Charles was thinking about his wife and daughter upstairs because he was confident his brothers were moving forward with the new plan. Paul made a compelling case and he would see everything through to the finish.

Paul stood and asked for an official vote.

Gene spoke first, "Let's just make it *hoodanimous*!"

They laughed at Gene's creative way of expressing a practical suggestion.

Paul confirmed. "Then it's settled."

Ronald, Byron, Gene and Charles nodded their heads in unison signaling agreement. Joseph stood and shook Paul's hand. "We are united."

The brothers cleaned up with practiced precision and packed up the leftovers. The gathering ended with handshakes and hugs as Charles led his brothers to his front door.

Joseph planned on taking a trip to a medical convention. He told his brothers he was staying over for a few extra days. "If there is anything you need call me." Joseph said. Paul told him. "We got it under control. Do ya thing Bro."

Gene winked and handed Charles two cuban cigars

sealed in cellophane wrapping. "Light one and hold one. Light one to celebrate Harper and we'll light up the other after we open our hood office." Charles laughed and tucked the cigars in his shirt pocket. "You got a deal," he said to his little brother.

Ronald parted with a reminder to Charles and Paul, "No matter what the city decides to do downtown, ECC has enough funding to purchase private property and the city can't do nothing about it!" They exchanged hugs then Ronald headed out the door.

Byron carried a paper plate filled with food wrapped tightly in aluminum foil. He paused in the doorway to thank Charles for the hospitality and congratulate him again before running to catch a ride with Ronald.

Paul was the last to leave. "You got y'self a beautiful wife and a healthy baby. Focus on Jo and Harper. I'll take over the business for a while."

"Thanks Bro, you know I appreciate it." Charles said gratefully.

"That's what brothers do," Paul said.

Charles accepted Paul's handshake and hug then closed and locked his front door.

New Moves

Paul transitioned easily into his role as the head of ECC. He asked Ron to review and revise the business plan along with the financials. He checked in with Charles and the plan was set in motion.

Paul told Ron and Gene at a follow-up meeting, "I suspect some crooked shit went down at city hall." Ronald agreed. "I feel you. I'm working on it."

"Okay report back to me. I'll relay it to Chay." Paul was being mindful not to distract Charles from his new fatherly duties unless absolutely necessary.

Ronald confirmed. "I'll work on getting more info while you keep it moving."

Gene said, "Right-on Bro. Solid."

Gene made contact with the neighborhood block captains and he visited the owner of the foster-home Paul and Charles renovated. The owner of the house was a long-time influencer in the neighborhood and the true heartbeat of the community. She was ageless and energetic. Gene met some of her kids; they all seemed happy. There was a piano in Mrs. Dunbar's living room; when the subject turned to music Gene offered to teach piano lessons to the children. Mrs. Dunbar was thrilled by the offer and gave her permission.

Gene reported, "The word is getting out with our people. The hood is looking forward to ECC's office relocation and community improvements."

The Ellisons set out on a course to uncharted territory executing their plan with Paul at the helm. There was nothing the city could do once ECC purchased the properties. The Ellisons legally owned lots, land and physical structures including abandoned properties sold to them by the original owners they tracked down.

ECC partnered with the Black and Brown community to develop an area long forgotten by the city. It took two years of perseverance and some finagling of the city's own processes. The Ellisons invited community leaders, city officials, commercial developers, politicians and the medical community to the grand opening of their new central office located in the newly named 'Spring Hill' district. The community hosted the ribbon-cutting ceremony. Charles and Joelle made their first official public appearance with two and half-year old Harper. Paul presented the project to the public and all six Ellison brothers cut the red, black and green ribbon to officially open the doors to the new Ellison Construction Company office. Gene and Mrs. Dunbar's children performed for the large crowd. There was full media coverage. Ellison Construction was the talk of the city. It was a brilliant move.

The following day the city news stations and newspapers reported on the event. The Philadelphia Tribune, the oldest African American newspaper in the United States, reported on the new construction.

"Spruce Hill District is a Triumph: An African-American family owned construction business, Ellison Construction, with six brothers forming the partnership, showed the power of leadership and collaboration yesterday. These Brothers partnered with an under served community to design, develop and build beautiful commercial, retail and residential properties in the city of their birth. They exemplify the City of Brotherly Love. The community transformation is miraculous. Ellison Construction opened their main office in the center of Spring Hill. Ellison Construction has made a positive impact on the city of Philadelphia. This home-grown family business did the city proud."

The Tribune featured a four-page spread with before and after photographs of the Spiring Hill Project. There were photos of the six ECC partners with a short biography for each. The other local newspapers also mentioned the new construction favorably.

Spring Hill was a victory for ECC and the Ellison family. It was an embarrassment for the city planners who never had the area on their development plans. It was a wake up call for those who used back door channels to acquire land and property; they felt cheated out of an opportunity. It was a problem for politicians who neglected the community. It was an insult to the ignorant who thought the Ellisons were new to the construction business; they lacked respect for the company and thought ECC was undeserving of the recognition. It was also more fuel for the bigots and racist in the city.

Paul was right, the success of the Spring Hill project put Ellison Construction on the city map. It also created more adversaries.

Shady Deals

Ronald Ellison spoke with his contacts in city hall. He discovered and confirmed through his resources the construction bid process was rigged. The long-standing process was built on nepotism and maintained through exclusion and unfair practices.

The city power-brokers put together a strategy to deliberately undermined Ellison Construction after the ManDane Library was presented to the public. A hospital board member leaked information to city officials ECC took on a major construction job without going through all the proper city channels. Calls were made to block ECC from all city construction projects.

Ronald also discovered Ellison Construction was not the only firm impacted by the illegal practice. Ronald obtained an official copy of a list of companies from another trusted source. Legitimate contracts were terminated illegally and some contractor licenses were being revoked by the corrupt officials using a system of 'pay to play.' The practice allowed developers and realtors to pay kick-backs to the officials in order to poach and snatch up properties. The city was holding onto abandoned houses in the poorer neighborhoods and lowering property values in the adjacent communities. City planners were recommending lenders, funding sources and grants to developers who bought into the system. The developers zeroed-in on lower income families. They offered them quick cash to get out of the blight but the offers were well below the real market value of their homes. Vacated homes were gutted, renovated and resold sometimes for ten-times over the original developer's purchase price. Some specific developers flipped over 95% of the communities they would never inhabit. Shady deals were going on and some city officials were benefiting. It was an unscrupulous network of crime and corruption.

Ronald said at the conclusion of his follow up report to Paul, "You called it Paul. Some shady stuff went down and it's still going down. The city was never going to let us build downtown."

Paul nodded in agreement. "Just like I thought."

Ronald added, "I asked Byron to notify the federal government. Federal funds were used on the projects. The Feds have an obligation to investigate all fraud, waste and abuse reports. There were also non-profit and minority funds set aside and we know the minority firms got the short end of the stick. They didn't tell us about the bid extension so you know they were not trying to tell us there was money and contracts on the table from the government allocated specifically for companies like ours. They purposely locked ECC out!"

Paul was thinking about Ron's approach to the problem. "So the Feds will expose the scandal, Smart Bro. I'll give the update to Chay. Watch your six."

Restart

Charles moved into the new Ellison headquarters in Spring Hill on Harper's third birthday. His office was large but it was cozy. Joelle bought a beautiful picture frame and inserted a photo of Harper for his desk. Things were going well and Joelle said she was ready for another baby. They were careful with birth control and finances. Charles spent some of his earnings on things for Joelle and Harper but he consulted with a financial planner and with Ronald's advice he was assured he had enough for Harper's education.

Joelle put three placemats on the conference table. Harper was on her knees in her Daddy's big chair leaning over his massive desk with paper and crayons. She was practicing the numbers and letters her Mommy wrote down for her.

"Babe I'm really proud of Paul. This place looks awesome." Joelle commented as she placed Harper's homemade birthday cake on the table along with colorful paper plates, forks and napkins.

Charles was proud of Paul too, but Charles was ready to retake the lead.

Joelle hugged him and reached up to touch his chin. "Don't worry about Paul, he's ready for this transition and so are you," she said.

Charles grinned because Joelle was always in tune with his thoughts. Charles lifted Joelle up off the floor. Harper squealed excitedly and scrambled out of the chair and ran to her father.

"Up Daddy," she said wanting to get in on the frolic. Joelle laughed down at Harper while Charles spun her around.

"I love you Joelle." Charles said as he snuggled into her shoulder then he put her back down to pick Harper up for a spin.

Towers Part 1 - Foundation

Chapter Five
PAUL - Riding the Wagon

Old Flame

Paul wrote a letter to ReeRee when he was in bootcamp. He figured out from her reply she was not in contact with her brother Rubin. ReeRee did not know about the circumstances that forced Rubin and Paul to enlist. Paul sent her another letter after he was deployed. He enclosed pictures of Okinawa, Japan and the sunset on the Saigon River in Vietnam. ReeRee sent a terse reply. She was in college focused on her studies and writing papers. She did not have time to write him letters. She had mixed feelings about the Vietnam War and the U. S. Invasion. She wrote he should have never joined the marines because he would be captured or killed in Vietnam. Paul decided it was best not to write any more letters to ReeRee.

Paul felt foolish for thinking maybe ReeRee would be waiting to welcome him home. He did not try to contact her since she never inquired about his return. He found out she graduated with a degree in social work, moved to an apartment in New Jersey and became a self-declared activist.

Paul was shocked when late one evening ReeRee showed up at his front door. It was six years since Paul last saw ReeRee. She was no longer the pretty teenage girl

Paul crushed on; Rita was a fine elegant woman. She explained her visit was about her brother. Paul invited her into his house.

"Rubin's been drifting since he got out the service. He's having trouble finding a job and when he does it's not consistent work. He started living on the streets. I tried to get him to move back into the house but he won't becauseI moved out the city. He told me he reenlisted." Rita was distraught, her hands shook as she wiped at her tears. She asked, "Why would he do that?"

Paul understood why Rubin reenlisted. Paul thought of his own situation. He spent all his service pay and if he did not have his family and the business he would be just like Rubin; unemployed, broke and trying to survive in America. Rita was Rubin's only family and she distanced herself from him over the years. Rubin made his own family in the Marine Corps.

Paul tried to comfort Rita. He ordered dinner and asked her to stay the night instead of traveling back over the bridge to her apartment. Rita agreed to stay.

Love and romance were not in the cards for Paul; in contrast to his younger brothers' busy social lives, Paul did not date. Paul considered himself damaged goods so he thought why would he subject anyone else to his problems. Rita tolerated him so he made the most out of the time they shared living together. Paul was close to happy. He was clean, working, contributing to his family's future and he was with Rita again.

Perfect Out

Paul did not have a lot of time to spend with Rita during the day. He was busy juggling his schedule; leading ECC; making critical business decisions; checking the construction sites; meeting with his brothers and reporting progress to Charles.

Then there were Paul's night terrors, long restless nights of tossing and turning in bed fighting an invisible enemy. One night he accidentally injured Rita. The blow left a large bruise on the side of her face and it took days to heal. She forgave him but she slept in the guest room after that night and she was wary whenever she was around him.

Rita refused to look at Paul while she packed her clothes in a duffle bag he gave her to use. Paul blocked the exit but he was not going to try to stop her from leaving. He expected her to leave him sooner. Paul did not know why Rita agreed to move in with him. He figured after she learned the truth about his enlistment she felt she owed him something because of her assumptions. Paul knew Rita did not love him. The Vietnam war was over and so was his relationship with Rita.

"Paul I can't do this no more. I just can't. You

never have time for me and now you're talking about taking on more work! I'm happy your business is going well. I'm happy about your brother's new baby and all that…but…I'm tired of always playing second to your family."

Paul watched Rita pack from the doorway without protest. It was true. Paul's family would always come first. This truth provided Rita the perfect out. Paul suspected Rita was already spending her time with someone else's family.

Rita removed her perfumes and lotions from the top of the dresser. She took up her silver bangle bracelets and slipped each one onto her wrist. The jingling sound and clink as each metal bracelet fell into place reminded Paul of the handcuffs the cops put on his wrists in the subway station. The entire scene felt like another bad turning point in his life. It turned out Paul was right.

Pressure Treatment

Paul took on the lead responsibly for ECC. He thought it was his duty to step up in order for Charles to spend time with Joelle and the new baby. He was grateful for the long hours and extra work, the business kept him from thinking about Rita and getting high.

Paul managed every detail of the Spring Hill District Project. He was determined to prove he could handle it all, but he was afraid he would not be able to live up to everyone's expectations. He worked relentlessly, some days he was so exhausted he was too tired to eat. Paul rose to the occasion, and in the end he delivered all he promised.

When Paul stood in front of the Spring Hill community and the public to represent the Ellison Construction Company he was emotional. He thanked all the partners, friends and family that contributed to the successful completion of the project.

After the ceremony Charles spoke to Paul privately "Pops and Mom are smiling on you today. I'm so proud of you Bro."

Paul was humbled. "I had great role models and mentors, including you Bro."

It was all Paul had a chance to say before they were

surrounded by the media and blinded by camera lights.

The successful opening of ECC's new corporate office in the Spring Hill District was a memorable day for Paul. He tried to be social but the praise he received about Spring Hill was overwhelming.

Paul welcomed Charles back and after the leadership transition was completed Paul had less work. Feeling his own purpose had diminished drove him to isolation. He was loosing the struggle to stay clean. No one knew because he was good at hiding his pain and suffering from everyone. Paul was putting everything in what he called his 'pressure cooker.' Paul used it to trap everything inside he struggled with in his life. It was filled with the remorse he felt for taking the lives of men; the aniexty of his unpredictable flashbacks; his chronic foot pain; his grief over the death of his father and mother and his loneliness without Rita. The internal pressure was building up in his pressure cooker. Paul needed a way to slowly release the pressure before it exploded.

New Woman

Visiting with Charles, Joelle and baby Harper impacted Paul in a way he never imagined. There was a small part of Paul that was envious of the fairytale life they seemed to share. Joelle was a loving wife. She loved being a mother and she supported the family. Joelle was the woman Paul thought Rita would become. He knew he was wrong for comparing the two women and wishing they were more alike. Rita was nothing like Joelle and Paul knew she would never measure up. Rita did not want a family. It made Paul sad his own relationship failed but he was genuinely happy for Charles and Joelle. Paul loved Harper like she was his own daughter, but his visits with her were a heartbreaking reminder of all the things missing in his own life.

Paul should have copped earlier but he worked the entire day. He went straight home and tried to ride it out but by midnight he knew it was going to be a rough night. He called ahead, then drove to the other side of the city to make his buy. He parked a block away then walked to the meet spot. His meeting place in the small park was full of late-night activity. Paul waited for his connection to arrive while he watched the young hustlers sell reefer.

They sat on concrete benches playing cards across a concrete table. Customers came and went after making their quick exchanges. Paul did not want what the young hustlers were selling.

Paul paced back and forth in the shadows. His meetings were becoming frequent but he never waited. His connection was not late, Paul was early. He knew he was on a binge and spiraling out of control but he could not stop. It was as if he was watching himself from outside his own body without any control over his actions. He went through the motions of a normal life but he was sneaking around at night and hiding his addiction from his family and employees during the day.

Paul did not feel he was 'off-the-wagon.' Paul felt like he hopped 'on-the-wagon.' He could not remember when he hopped on but now the wagon was moving too fast for him to hop off. He was riding the wagon into oblivion to kill all the pain in his soul. A little something to help him through the nights quieted his physical pain and suppressed the painful memories of his past.

He still yearned for the slow dance with heroin, his brown woman. Paul enjoyed the heavy stoned feeling that settled around his head when he shot her into the veins of his feet or snorted her through his nostrils. Times changed. Paul replaced his brown woman with a white woman. Cocaine stimulated him and made him feel invincible. She was a fast dancer. He snorted her, then learned to smoke her because she was better when she was hot. He ate and drank her too. She kept him up and she never made him feel low. She was expensive but Paul had plenty of money so he could afford to keep his new woman happy. Paul waited anxiously for her to show up with her escort.

Daymares

Paul's orders were to identify the dead. He saw scorched and incinerated human body parts, some were almost unrecognizable. His fallen comrades were in burned and bloody chunks strewn around the battle fields and marsh. Paul collected the military identification tags they called dog-tags from the dead bodies. He also collected dismembered limbs, fingers, toes and heads. He dropped them into bags carrying out his orders. Paul wondered who would be ordered to pick up his pieces. He found his own body. It was bloody, bullet riddled and burned but he knew it was his; he saw his birthmark on the blistered flesh of the arm, his dead hand clenched his M-16... the bayonet was missing. Paul marched on his bare feet through wet slimy marshland. Snakes, leeches and other slimy crawling creatures feasted on his exposed flesh. He looked down into the murky waters. The flesh on his feet was eaten away, the skeletal bones were carrying his weight. He kept marching on his bones. He marched through thick yellow smoke that made his eyes burn. He smelled sulfur and cordite on the air from heavy artillery fire. He smelled burned flesh from the putrid decaying bodies floating in the polluted swamp and he felt like vomiting.

Paul's dream dissolved into his reality. He opened his eyes expecting to see the blue textured ceiling of his bedroom the place where he usually woke from the horrors in his nightmares; instead he saw peeling paint and dangling plaster hanging perilously above his head. He was spread eagle on a mattress flattened against the floor. He smelled sweat and urine, but it was better than what he smelled in his nightmare. He sat up slowly in an unfamiliar room filled with unfamiliar people sprawled around sleeping, shaking and smoking. His expensive shoes were missing but he still had socks and flesh on his feet. He actually wished the thief removed his socks to see his scarred and mangled size sixteens; it would have blown his high. He struggled to stand up then stumbled over to a wall. The dark room was illuminated by the occasional flicker and flame of lighters. He fell over something on the floor. He pushed his weight up and off of it. It was a man. The man never moved but his eyes were open and he mumbled as he stared into space. There were others around him laid out in drug induced stupors. Paul continued to crawl across the floor commando style. He reached a corner and used the wall to help stand up again. There was a chemical smell mixed with filth and disease. It reminded Paul of the bad days in Nam. He vomited in the corner of a cracked wall. No one noticed. He inched his way around the room searching for an exit. He found the front door and twisted the broken doorknob. It opened easily. He walked out of the dark dilapidated house shielding his eyes from the bright sunlight. He sat on the front steps breathing in the outdoor air thankful he escaped from hostile territory.

Intervention

Joseph asked Charles to meet him at the medical building. Charles thought it was a peculiar request since everything was already moved out to the new ECC headquarters in Spring Hill. As soon as Charles arrived Joseph took him into his private office and spoke with urgency. "Paul's on something, I'm hoping I'm wrong but my guess is it's cocaine or some other stimulant. I can't be certain. Have you noticed any changes in his behavior?" Joseph waited for Charles to think before he answered.

Charles sat in the chair across from Joseph's desk. He thought about how busy he was with Joelle and Harper. The years passed in the blink of an eye, Charles was focused on his wife, his child and building his home. After Paul reported Spring Hill was completed, Charles realized nearly three years passed. He jumped in ready to take back his responsibilities from Paul. Charles was able to achieve balance between his family and the business and Paul was still the same great partner. Charles did not expect to see Paul in the office after the leadership transition because Paul preferred to work at the construction sites. The last time Charles saw Paul he noticed he loss weight. When Paul started leaving for long weekends he told Charles his workload was lighter and he was taking some time to himself. Charles thought it was a great idea because Paul deserved time off after he assumed temporary leadership of ECC for over three years and successfully completed the Spring Hill project. Sitting in Joseph's office thinking about his question made Charles realize he really did not know what was going on in Paul's personal life.

Brothers & Friends

Charles asked Rubin, "Have you seen Paul?"

"Nah Bro, I figured he been busy workin. We talked over the phone but I ain't seen him since I got back out. I saw him in the Tribune though. Shiiiit y'all blowing up. What's up?" Rubin asked.

Charles explained. "I'm worried, so is Joe. We can't reach him and it looks like he hasn't been at his house in days. We think he might be somewhere doing drugs."

There was silence between the two men on the phone as they each thought about all the reasons why Paul might turn to drugs.

Rubin understood it best. He chased the dragon and he knew what the ride was like, he made a narrow escape before the dragon turned to chase him. He offered to help. "Chay, I might know where he is. I'm at Manny's, can you pick me up?"

Manny's was a popular twenty-four hour soul food diner. Charles was there in less than ten minutes.

Charles drove to various locations in unfamiliar neighborhoods while Rubin gave directions. They found Paul without his shoes passed out on the front steps of an abandoned and boarded up house. Rubin said it was a drug addict haven. Charles and Rubin woke him and pulled him up from the steps. Paul kept mumbling about a pressure cooker. Charles held him up. Rubin went into the house to find Paul's shoes. He came right back out.

"I found his jacket and shoes, probably cause caint' nobody fit em'. No wallet or watch though. Shiiit he can forget about them." Rubin dropped Paul's custom made size sixteen British style oxfords in the back of the truck then helped Charles push Paul into the back seat. Rubin fastened Paul's seat belt securely. He used Paul's suit jacket to cover him before he got in the front seat with Charles. "Shiiiit Man, Paulie needs professional help and he's got to want it. We can't make him get clean." Rubin said wisely.

Charles started the truck but instead of pulling off he turned to Rubin. "I need you to stay with Paul at his place for a while. I know it's a lot to ask but Joe's gonna help. I know you're working on fixing your house. You can use Paul's place as a cot and squat until your house is in shape."

Rubin sucked his teeth. "Shiiiit Man, I wanted to called y'all but I can't afford supplies. The car repair shop moved or went outta business or something...I don't know...but I couldn't find no work till I got this bull-shit job. Manny's don't pay much but I get free meals and it keeps me out of trouble." Rubin looked at Paul slumped in the back seat of the truck passed out with drool hanging from his lip. Rubin turned to Charles. "Shiiiit we both got wounds. I remember the old days. Paulie always had my back even when I ain't deserve it. I'll stay with him if he let me." Charles squeezed Rubin's shoulder. He said, "Thanks man, you've always been like a brother to all of us. I'm glad your're here. I think it's divine intervention." Rubin said, "Shiiiit, we gonna see what the fuck Paulie thinks about that."

Rubin made Charles laugh despite the gravity of the situation.

Charles helped Rubin move into Paul's house. Charles refused to put Paul in a hospital. Joseph said they would only treat him with methadone or some other drugs. He said Paul would just be hooked on something else with another side-effect.

Rubin thought Charles and Joseph wanted to avoid the bad publicity because Paul's addiction would cause a shit-storm for the Ellison family and their business. Rubin soon realized he was wrong. He saw how much Paul meant to all his brothers. They surrounded Paul with protection and rallied around him to nurse him back to health. Joseph visited Paul daily to monitor his progress while assisting as much as he could to manage Paul's withdrawal. Charles kept Paul well fed and his fridge stocked. Ronald paid all Paul's bills and made sure his bank accounts and investments were secured. Gene bought music over to lift Paul's spirits and when Paul needed to talk about his feelings Byron provided an ear for Paul to talk. Joelle helped too; when Paul was able she asked him to join her with Harper for short strolls through the house garden.

Rubin became closer to Paul and the Ellison Brothers as Paul recovered. He felt privileged to be a part of the Ellison family. Rubin lived with Paul for a year. Paul helped Rubin finish the renovations in his house and the work helped Paul maintain his sobriety.

Chapter Six
CHARLES - The Expansion

Sydney Marie Ellison

Joelle's labor with her second child was not as dramatic as it was with her first. The contractions started and there was no paralysis or need for an ambulance. Joelle simply told Charles to get the car because the baby was coming. Charles took control and carefully escorted Joelle out of a charity event. He told the valet to make it quick, it was the only time he raised his voice. Joelle squeezed his hand affectionately at first until she felt another contraction. The discomfort made her squeeze his hand so tight it made Charles grimace. The car arrived in short-order. Charles tipped the valet with a hundred-dollar bill. The young man thanked him, and shoved it in his shirt pocket to assist them into their vehicle.

They arrived at the hospital eighteen minutes before the birth. Charles was relieved Joelle was okay. He was freaked-out when she fainted shortly after they cut the cord but the nurse revived her immediately. The thought of loosing Joelle in childbirth was a reminder to Charles of the fragility of life. He would never forget the joy he felt at the birth of his first child; now, looking at his second child, Charles felt blessed twice over. He watched the new little miracle wiggle and squirm as the nurse checked her over and cleaned her up for him to hold.

Charles carried his second daughter to his exhausted but excited wife. He placed her delicately in Joelle's outstretched arms. "She looks just like Harper!" he said. Joelle was delighted when she saw her newborn's little face.

"Oh Charles look she has your cleft!" Joelle started to cry. Charles dropped down to the side of the hospital bed and asked, "What's wrong? Are you in pain? Should I get the nurse?"

Joelle shook her head. She said, "There's absolutely nothing wrong. These are happy tears. I have two healthy beautiful daughters because of loving you." Joelle pulled Charles closer. Charles kissed her then kissed his new baby girl.

Earlier in the year Joelle suggested they take a real family vacation with Harper. She spoke about Australia. "The summer is our winter. I have my summer break and you can schedule some time off then." Charles thought it was an excellent idea and an interesting destination. They planned their family's first trip out of the country but the trip was postponed when they found out Joelle was expecting their second child. They were not disappointed the trip to Australia was canceled; instead they made plans to welcome Sydney into the family, it became the perfect name choice for a boy or girl.

Charles whispered, "Hello Sydney Marie Ellison." He was enchanted with his new little princess. She was a match to her older sister with an added cleft. He planted a soft kiss on her tiny hand; then hurried to the hospital waiting room to get his other princess so she could meet her little sister.

Little Sister

Harper waited with her Uncle Doctor Joe while her Mommy and Daddy helped her little sister 'be born.' Harper could not wait to see a living babydoll they could bring home for her to keep. Her mother told her big sisters were special and very important for little sisters; she said Harper would show Sydney the ropes. Harper thought it was funny because she did not think a little baby could jump rope. Her mother explained Harper would be her little sister's teacher and teachers always made sure students learned new things. Harper understood because Mommy was a teacher and Harper learned new things from her everyday.

Harper told her mother, "I'm going to be a good teacher for my little sister. She's going to be smart like me." When Harper saw how small her new baby sister was she admitted, "I don't know how to teach a baby."

Harper saw how the tiny baby's long eyelashes covered her eyes while she slept in her mother's arms. Sydney sucked on her own tongue. Harper liked the dimple in her chin, it looked like her Daddy's. Harper thought the baby was cute but she was too little to play with. Harper looked up at her parents and told them in very serious tone, "I'm going to be a good big sister because Sydney is only zero right now. I'm going to teach her how to grow like me so she can play. She's going to learn fast." Harper smiled at Sydney.

Charles and Joelle marveled at Harper's wisdom. Charles bent down and scooped Harper up in his arms. He kissed her cheeks and her neck. Harper squealed and giggled until he put her down because Daddy's kisses under her neck tickled.

Harper climbed on the side of the hospital bed. Her Daddy stood next to the bed towering above them all. Harper watched closely as her mother lifted the baby's shirt to adjust something. Harper frowned when she saw her sister's belly button. There was a large white plastic clamp on it. Harper's protective instincts for her sister were already developing. There was anxiety in Harper's voice as she looked at her sister sympathetically. Harper wanted her mother to explain. "Mommy why did they put a clothespin on Sydney's stomach?"

Joelle calmed Harper with a soft tone and soothing words. "Don't worry Honey. She's fine. It doesn't hurt. It's the umbilical cord, it connected us and allowed me to feed her while she was inside my tummy. Sydney doesn't need it any more. The doctor put the clamp on so Sydney will have a cute little belly button like yours."

Joelle watched Harper's expression change from concern to curiosity. Harper seemed satisfied with her mother's explanation but when the doctor and nurse returned to the room, Harper narrowed her eyes into tiny little accusatory slits and there was a scowl on her face. Her eyes followed their every move until they left the room. Charles and Joelle were amused by Harper's behavior.

Charles and Joelle were new to being parents of two children but they were confident together they could manage their growing family. Charles and Joelle wanted to raise healthy children so in anticipation of having their second child they read books written by child psychologists describing the complications of sibling rivalry and behaviors that could occur when children were born close together. They heard the first-born might feel left out as the newborn received all the attention. They read some scary stuff could happen if the first-born child never adjusted to the new sibling.

Charles, one of six siblings, thought it was

interesting but he felt it depended on how the siblings were raised. He said he and Paul was born in the same year and there was never any rivalry between them. He told Joelle his brothers were raised to support each other and work as a unit, rivalry was never a part of his family dynamics.

Joelle never had a sibling so she was especially relieved when they observed Harper with her sister for the very first time. Harper did not manifest any of the warning signs or red-flag behaviors they read about indicating there was going to be a problem.

Harper was helpful and she gave Sydney more attention than anyone else except Joelle. Harper was all over her little sister everyday and all day. Joelle asked Harper on many occasions to leave Sydney alone so she could sleep. Harper would object and Joelle would eventually give in because Sydney always cried out for Harper to return. Harper was always ready with more funny faces, tickles and kisses for her little sister.

Joelle knew her daughters would grow to love and protect each other but Joelle would never witness how strong Harper and Sydney's love and protection for one another would become.

Dr. Duemijon-Ellison

Dr. Joelle Duemijon-Ellison's first priority was her family. She rearranged her schedule to accommodate the new family dynamics. A wife, mother of two and a professional educator; she was a master at multitasking. She continued working at the school for the gifted and tutoring, but she spent most of her hours homeschooling her girls.

Joelle started teaching her children at an early age. She taught them languages, math, science, literature and physics. Harper and Sydney were reading, writing and calculating problems far ahead of the standard developmental stages. They were both extremely intelligent and curious.

Joelle took Harper and Sydney every where she went, it was built into her schedule. If Joelle was teaching at the school her children were in the class; when she presented curriculums. Harper and Sydney sat quietly with the audience and watched her slideshows; when she took them to the weekly children's reading circle at the ManDane hospital library it became their favorite place to visit. They spent hours in the library picking out books and reading with other children. The girls made lots of friends at the hospital.

"Charles I think it's time to send the girls to school." Joelle said one night before bed.

Charles asked, "Why would they want to go to a regular school when they have the best teacher right here?" Charles was so accustomed to his wife teaching the girls it never occurred to him his children would leave their home to attend a school with other teachers. They had their own little custom built school house on the grounds. It was a gift from their uncle and now official God father Paul.

He watched his wife prepare for bed. Every time Charles laid his eyes on Joelle he thought she was more beautiful and after having two children somehow she seemed to glow brighter. She stuck her tongue out at him in the mirror when she caught him looking.

"Babe the girls need to socialize and become their own little people." Joelle explained as she tied a satin scarf around her hair. She gave him a peck on the cheek after she finished and hopped into their king-sized platform bed.

The girls were in their separate bedrooms asleep.

Charles did not want to admit his girls were growing up. Harper was six and Sydney would soon turn three. Charles could not believe how fast time was flying. He thought back to the first time he saw Joelle. She did make a good mother just like he knew she would.

Charles pulled the covers over them then pulled Joelle into their favorite spooning position. He traced the contours of her curves while she spoke. "I've always dreamed of opening my own school," Joelle said and snuggled closer.

Charles wanted to help fulfill his wife's dreams. He was supportive. "Okay Dr. Duemijon-Ellison, I'll build one for you. If my brother can build a little school by himself, I'm sure with some help I can build a big one."

Chapter Seven

PAUL - Second Chance

M. I. A.

Paul found himself outside another drug house penniless and missing his shoes again, he guessed the desperate were not scared of his ugly feet this time; they probably saw worse. He came off a long ride and now he was thirsty and hungry. He only knew one place to turn. He walked to the corner on his disfigured bare feet to get to the phone booth illuminated by the a street light. He dialed "0" to place a collect call.

Joelle answered. "Hello."

She heard a series of mechanical clicks and then a polite woman's voice spoke. "I have a collect call from Paul Ellison for Charles Ellison Jr. will you accept the charges?"

Joelle answered without hesitation. "Yes, I'll accept."

Charles was upstairs tucking the girls in for the night. Joelle waited anxiously for the operator to connect the call. She heard the same series of clicks before the operator asked in a pleasant voice. "Would you like to establish a credit account for this call?"

Joelle was annoyed; she knew the operator's tactic was to keep her on the line longer to purposely run up more charges. Joelle told the operator in a curt voice.

"Look this must be an emergency."

The operator's tone was still polite but she spoke faster. "Go ahead sir your party is on the line. Thank you for using TelCom." There was a final click when the operator dropped off the line.

Joelle looked toward the staircase hoping Charles was on his way down to the first floor. "Paul, what's going on?" Joelle waited anxiously for his response.

Paul was unsteady on his bad feet and his speech was slurred. He sobbed into the phone, "I'm ssorry Jo. I need to speak to Chay. I mm..messssed up."

Joelle heard desperation in Paul's voice. She was afraid he might hang up. She asked "Where are you Paul?"

Paul was crammed inside a phone booth he was too tall to fit in. He hit his head against the metal ceiling light twice before he bent his knees to shorten himself. Leaning his back against the scarred graffiti covered plexiglass window he clutched the phone receiver. "I'm in hell," he said.

Joelle ran up the stairs with the cordless handset. She told Paul, "Hold on. Please don't hang up, I'm going to get Charles."

Paul repeated over and over, "Ssssorry…I'm…so

sorry, I'm…sorry."

Charles was on the phone. "Hey Bro. What's up?"

Paul began to weep when he heard his brother's voice. He fell to his knees in despair. He hit rock-bottom. He needed and wanted help out of his destructive cycle. Paul begged for sanctuary. "I need help, I fucked up. I fucked up bad Bro."

Charles beckoned Joelle to his side and held her close. Joelle nudged under her husband's shoulder. "Give me your location," he said into the phone. Joelle started to cry when she heard Paul crying as he gave Charles his location. Charles planted a kiss on her forehead while he spoke to Paul. "Okay, I know the corner. Stay there. I'm coming."

Charles pushed the end button on the phone and looked into his wife's eyes. Joelle's eyes were filled with compassion.

Rescue

Paul could have called any one of his brothers, he knew they would come but he only wanted his big brother, his Irish twin. When he saw Charles through the dirty window of the phone booth he knew he was saved. Charles helped him out of the narrow square box into a wide circle of love.

Paul checked himself into rehab with Charles and Joseph standing by his side; his other three brothers were waiting to hear word. Joseph assured him the rehabilitation center was private and discreet. Paul was grateful because he did not want his addiction to go public; he knew it would negatively impact the family and the business. He also knew it was not going to be easy to get clean again, but he was determined to get his life back on track. Paul spent ninety days in the rehabilitation facility.

Charles and Joelle asked Paul to move into their home. They had more than enough space to accommodate him and he would still have privacy. Joelle told him he needed to earn her trust, but she was willing to let him stay if he was willing to truly commit himself to staying healthy. She made it clear she would not tolerate drugs in her home and she warned him there would be no second chances.

Paul fully understood the consequences if he went back on his word. He was appreciative of his brother and sister-in law's kindness. He loved them and he was devoted to his nieces. Harper and Sydney were part of the reason Paul knew he would keep his word to Joelle.

Paul gained weight with the help of Charles and Joelle's healthy and delicious meals. He was physically fit again from workouts with Ron. It felt good being healthy again, he felt better than he had in decades. He was still an addict but he felt more like his old self, plus a few ten years and minus the drugs.

Paul made funny faces at little Sydney from across the dinner table. Harper was holding the knife and fork in the wrong position trying to cut up her food. Paul put his own fork and knife down to help Harper. He switched around her child-sized utensils and placed them in her hands. She looked bewildered. Paul picked up his own knife and fork in the correct position and demonstrated on his own plate how to cut the food on her plate. Harper followed his example and achieved success. She smiled proudly. Sydney smiled too because Harper was smiling.

Paul winked at Sydney, "Please pass the butter

Syd." Sydney laughed at the name uncle Paul called her then she informed her uncle, "Momma calls me Nee-Nee."

Joelle helped Sydney pass the butter dish to Paul. She asked him, "Have you decided when you're going back to work?"

An awkward silence passed between the three adults. Joelle looked embarrassed. Paul knew she meant well, she was only trying to move things along.

Charles touched Joelle's hand and broke the silence. "Jo leave the man alone while he's buttering his biscuits."

"It's cool Bro, Jo is right. I need to take the next step toward reclaiming my life." Paul said. Then Paul answered Joelle's question. "I decided it's time for me to get back to work. I missed it and I'm ready!"

It was clear to Joelle Paul regained his confidence. There was also gratitude in Paul's expression. Charles looked away but not before Joelle saw a tear in his eye. Paul saw his brother's tear too so he lightened the mood. He reached over and grabbed another biscuit. "I better eat some more of these cause I'm gonna need energy," Paul said. Charles confirmed, "You know it Bro, cause we start tomorrow."

Joelle watched the two brothers execute a rhythmic pattern of hand holds, palm slaps and fist bumps in their ritual handshake. Harper and Sydney tried to duplicate the handshake but they turned it into the pat-a-cake clapping game. Paul laughed at Harper and Sydney.

There were many good things in Paul's life and he was not going to take them for granted any longer. He was given another chance to live it right. Paul was on the two hundred and sixty-seventh day of his sobriety.

Chapter Eight
CHARLES - Unexpected Results

Build Out

Charles continued to make good decisions as CEO of Ellison Construction and Development. His life was charmed. All his hard work with his brothers was finally paying off and his ship was sailing in. He had a beautiful family and they were financially secure. It was time to make a few bold moves, it was the Ellison way.

Charles wanted to reach out to Caribbean countries. He was interested in their building techniques and disaster recovery methods. The possibility of ECC building partnerships across the islands to construct resorts, villas and spas was appealing.

Gene and Byron spent vacations in the Caribbean, they were all in for international expansion. Joseph made frequent visits to Italy, he had never been to Jamaica but he thought it was a great place to start. Ronald said it could be lucrative for the company and Jamaica was worth exploring since the resort business was growing and the Jamaican exchange rate was in U. S. favor. Paul said he was going to soak his feet in the Caribbean sea while they were on the trip.

Joelle joked with her husband, "Charles you should take the trip with your brothers. I need a testosterone break."

Charles told Joelle, "It's going to take a lot of work getting through the government's red tape to execute this international endeavor. It might take years, so…. in the meantime, we're going to build you a school."

The plan was for ECC to complete the Duemijon School construction by the end of the summer in time for a fall opening. It was Charles' last official hands-on project before taking an administrative role in the company. He planned to take his family to visit the Caribbean once the school was open.

They were still on schedule with the construction but the weather was not helping the situation. It was the hottest summer on record for Philadelphia. Heatwave after heatwave hit the city. The construction materials absorbed the heat and the concrete temperature was well over one hundred degrees.

Charles monitored the heat advisories and paced himself along with the crew. There was a heat related incident at the school construction site. A crew member nearly passed out from dehydration and heat exhaustion. He wobbled over to the watering station and after confirming he was okay, Charles dismissed him and the rest of the crew for their safety. He remained at the site for a walk-through to inspect their progress. Satisfied and proud of the quality of the work from his crew, he grabbed his water thermos and called home to check on his family.

Harper was the first to snatch up the phone. Charles could hear Sydney shouting at Harper. "I want ta speak to Daddy too! Daaaadddy!"

Charles spoke to Harper. "Hey Princess, what are you and Sydney doing?"

Charles chuckled when instead of an answer, he heard a tussle over the phone followed by Joelle's muffled voice coaxing the girls to settle down. Charles closed his eyes and pictured Harper and Sydney dancing around Joelle reaching for the phone.

Joelle sounded tired. "Hey Babe."

Charles responded, "Hello My Love. How y'all making out in this heat? Is the air on?"

Joelle knew her man well, he was always more concerned about others than himself. "Yes the air is on and we're fine in the house. It's too hot out there. These temperatures are dangerous. I know you already let the crew go. I'm worried about you now. Come home."

Charles took off his hard-hat, drank the entire thermos of water and wiped the sweat from his brow with his bandana. Joelle was right, it was too hot and he was beginning to feel the effects. He told her he was heading straight home.

A Promise

Illness and death sometimes comes without any warning. It sneaks in during the spring while you smell the well tended flowers in your garden and you and your wife make new plans for an international trip with your children. It is invisible as you discuss activity ideas with your wife, who is a little too excited about having a couples manicure and pedicure. It comes quietly while you listen to your wife's enthusiastic chatter about shopping and walking on the beach. It comes knowing you are unaware the trip will never happen.

The Caribbean trip was finalized. Joelle told Charles she experienced some light-headiness so she scheduled an appointment with the doctor to check things out before the trip. She asked him to drive her as a precaution and to call one of his brothers to watch the girls. Charles was secretly hoping the dizziness meant Joelle was pregnant again. He thought having a son would be more icing on their cake. Charles drove Joelle to the appointment anticipating they would need to delay another trip to have a baby.

Joelle's primary doctor was cordial and full of good humor. She performed some tests and after the tests were completed her demeanor changed. The doctor was extremely concerned. She told Charles in a quiet comforting tone of voice she would be admitting Joelle into the hospital. Her office was already coordinating with a hospital medical team. Charles began to panic as the medical office staff moved with lightening speed.

Joelle was placed in a wheelchair and they were escorted by a physician's assistant over to the adjacent hospital through a series of connected corridors and elevators. The hospital was prepared for Joelle's arrival. They put her on a stretcher and immediately raced her to a special examining room. Charles held her hand while leaning down over the rolling, rattling bed.

After more tests, Charles sat beside Joelle on a hospital bed in a private room He held her hand rubbing her ring finger and wedding band with his thumb. She insisted on keeping the ring on after a nurse told her to undress and remove all jewelry for hospital admission. Joelle was emphatic that she was not going to remove her wedding band. She raised her voice and snapped at the nurse. "No! I never take my wedding ring off!" She told Charles. "I'm not taking it off, you tell her I never take it off!"

The nurse was sympathetic. She thought the woman should be able to do whatever she wanted. The nurse spent many years in neurology. The patient's preliminary test results and images indicated there was severe brain trauma. The nurse thought it was a wonder the woman was still coherent. The nurse saw it before, it would take a miracle for the patient to fully recover. The nurse ignored the hospital admission rules about jewelry. She left the couple alone and prayed for a miracle.

Joelle looked up at Charles as if she had a question, then her expression turned into a blank stare and her hand went limp in his grasp.

Charles stood aside and watched helplessly as a nurse expertly punctured Joelle's arm and inserted an IV. She hung a plastic bag filled with clear fluid on a hook behind the pole connected to a new stationary bed. She left the room quietly. Two other female nurses entered; one politely showed Charles where to stand so he could observe without interference. The nurses began to work together. One nurse removed Joelle's ring and handed it to Charles. Joelle was not able to protest. The other nurse put Joelle's dress on a hanger and placed it in the built-in closet next to the medical equipment and machines. Charles noticed Joelle wore the dress he gave her for

Mother's Day. The nurses were efficient and respectful as they removed Joelle's undergarments and adjusted the hospital gown around her limp body. They stuck four plastic adhesive discs above her bare breast and arranged the cords to properly connect her to the monitoring machine. They made a final inspection of the wires on the equipment then tied Joelle's hospital gown with the opening in the front. Charles wanted to tie the ribbons more securely to protect Joelle's modesty. The nurse pressed a button on the machine and he jumped when it beeped. He looked at the wires and tubes connected to his wife as she sunk back into the bed gently snoring. The nurse went about her routine, taking vital signs and adjusting the flow of the dripping fluid. A young man came in and adjusted the machine's volume and other controls; he gave Charles a nod and left without speaking.

It was as if time jumped ahead when Joelle's doctor and another attending specialist pulled him away. Charles was in a state of shock. The specialist looked somber when he said, "Mr. Ellison, please let us try to help her, the neurosurgeon is here."

Joelle was rushed into surgery while Charles waited in the cold sterile hospital room. Hours later a new doctor entered the room. She asked him to step out and hastened him into the hallway before he could object. A male nurse rolled Joelle back into the room. She was still asleep but now all her hair was shaved off and a large bandage covered her head. The surgeon gave an update about Joelle's condition. "Mrs. Ellison has suffered multiple strokes, what we call brain hemorrhages. The strokes caused severe tears in her brain resulting in a major aneurysm. She is no longer showing any neurological response. The damage was impossible to repair. I'm so sorry."

Charles asked while peeping through the door's thick windowpane as the male nurse shifted Joelle gently back onto the hospital bed. "What are you saying? What does that mean? What's happening? I don't understand. What's wrong with my wife?" Charles stared at the new doctor. "My wife had a dizzy spell. She had them before when she was pregnant. This is crazy. She just needs rest." Charles pointed to the IV tube with frustration. "What are you giving her?" he asked then demanded, "Give her something else to wake her up!"

The surgeon waited patiently for Charles to collect himself then explained.

"There is nothing else we can give. The hemorrhages

were severe. Her brain is swelling. The IV fluid is to reduce the swelling although her brain has already shut down and there is no longer any activity. Soon the other organs will begin to fail. The vital organs cannot survive without a functioning brain." She paused to allow Charles to process what she said before she continued. "We ran tests again and re-analyzed the images. We were able to relieve some of the pressure during surgery but we can not repair or reverse the damage; it was too extensive. The brain is a complex organ. We probably won't know what really happened until we conduct an aut....."

The surgeon stopped talking when she saw Charles was crying. She opened the door to the room. Charles entered the room and the male nurse exited. A clear plastic mask covered Joelle's nose. An odd green accordion tube was taped to her lip and sticking out of her mouth, it was connected to new machine; it made soft whooshing noises along side the other beeping machine. Charles seemed calm but the surgeon noticed his fists were clenched. She read Joelle's paperwork attached to a clipboard and pulled out a pen from her jacket pocket. She spoke softly to Charles, "I'm sure you are aware Mrs. Ellison has an Advanced Directive and is listed as an organ donor. Her directive has specific DNR orders and her desire is to end artificial life-support if an unfortunate event like this ever happened." The surgeon pointed toward the machine with her pen then to Joelle. She was empathetic. "I know this is hard, but please understand we must honor the patient's wishes. There is no brain activity and the machine is breathing for her; without the machine her life will end. There's a long list of eligible patients waiting for her gifts." Charles did not respond. He stared at the machine. The surgeon moved closer to Charles to force him to make eye contact. She wanted to be sure he heard her clearly. "Charles we need your signature on the forms to disconnected Joelle from life support." She placed her hand over his to comfort him. "Joelle would have wanted you to act as soon as possible."

The surgeon's face was familiar, Charles saw her before at hospital fundraisers. Things were fuzzy since they arrived at the hospital, he realized he knew her. Looking into her eyes bought him back to the present and out of his denial. He read the name tag pinned on the pocket of the jacket over her scrubs. 'Dr. V, Coleman,' he tried to recall her first name. *Was his brain shutting down too? Yes, he knew his wife was an organ donor. He learned about the donor program from his wife. He was an organ donor too because of his wife. Yes, he knew Joelle would want him to act*

ASAP. Dr. Coleman, whose first name he could not remember, was right. He needed to sign the forms, he needed to act as soon as possible. There were other people who could benefit from Joelle's gifts. She would have wanted to help others.

Charles squeezed into the small chair next to the bed to hold Joelle's hand. There was a breathing tube down her throat connected to the machine breathing for her to keep her alive. He rubbed his thumb against the wedding band he placed back on her finger. He kissed her mouth and touched her face. He asked God to take her until it was his turn to reunite with her again.

Charles signed the necessary paperwork and notified her parents. He waited for the Duemijons to arrive with his brothers Joseph and Byron to witness Joelle's passing. Gene was on tour with his band. Harper and Sydney were at home with Paul. His daughters were unaware their father was performing the undesirable task of preparing himself for their mother's death.

Ten hours, one exploratory and repair surgery and two strokes since they visited the doctor's office, Charles sat in the sanctum of the small hospital room alone with Joelle. He did not see Dr. Coleman enter the room behind him but he heard her footsteps and he felt the air shift as others followed in behind the doctor.

Charles never turned around, his eyes were fixed on Joelle witnessing her final moments. He shifted his gaze from his wife's peaceful face to the monitor. He watched the steady LED light pattern form a bright green neon line of little inverted V's. He never saw them remove the tube from her mouth. He heard a click and the whooshing sound stopped abruptly. He heard another click and a straight steady line trailed across the screen.

Plans for their future were ending. Plans to have more children; ^^__^^_ plans to build additions on their house; ^^__^^_ plans to watch the girls grow into women; ^^__^^_ plans to spoil their grandchildren; ^___^^_ plans to retire; __^__^____ plans to travel; _____^____ and plans to grow old together were ended in a final straight neon green line......._____.

Charles turned his attention back to his beautiful sleeping wife. He thanked Joelle for the love she shared with him. He thanked her for accepting him with all of his faults. He thanked her for bringing their children into the world and making him a father. He thanked her for taking care of the family including his brothers. He said he was sorry they were not together for as long as they hoped. He stood over her hospital bed and thanked God for sending Joelle to him, then he recited the Lord's

Prayer. Voices joined in and finished the prayer. Charles removed Joelle's wedding band from her finger. He leaned down to whisper a promise into her ear. Then Charles kissed Joelle one last time. Joelle inhaled to accept his kiss and for a fleeting moment Charles imagined he awakened his sleeping beauty, but when Joelle exhaled it was her last breath. Her light was extinguished and her glow was gone. Charles put her wedding band in his pocket and wept.

Heavenly Sleepova

"Your Mommy has gone to sleep and when she wakes up she will be with the angels."

Harper looked at her father with skepticism. She put down the bedtime story she was reading to Sydney and asked suspiciously, "Who are these angels?" She pointed to Sydney and to herself and with conviction she told her father, "Mommy said *we* are her angels."

Sydney, dressed in her favorite pajamas clutched her dolly dressed in a miniaturized matching nightgown. She looked at her father in confusion. She asked, "Is momma coming back afer her sleepova?"

Charles wanted to explain further but when he looked into the eyes of his little girls he could not find the appropriate words. How could he explain death to a nine and six-year old? He wanted to cry because Joelle would have known exactly what to say.

Harper and Sydney waited for him to say something. Charles tried to control his emotions as he sat down beside them on the plush carpet. He pushed the book aside and positioned himself on the floor with his girls.

He focused on Sydney first. "No, Sydney, Momma can't come home," he said then he turned to Harper. He choked on his words. "Harper, she's with the angels in heaven." He could not say anything more, he buried his face in his large hands and cried like he was a child.

The girls did not understand exactly what happened but they understood Daddy was sad and needed a hug. They both encircled their arms around him. Two arms around his neck and two arms around his waist squeezed and held him tight. Harper and Sydney knew Daddy and Mommy liked to *feel* hugs. They were going to double up Daddy's *feeling* hugs because Mommy was not coming back from her sleepover with the angels in heaven.

Charles held his girls and rocked them back and forth as he felt the waves of despair and grief wash over him. Finally, able to regain his composure, he kissed his children and gathered them into his arms. He carried them up the staircase to their adjoining bedrooms. He decided to place them both in Harper's bed.

Harper surprised him when she asked, "Daddy can we say a special prayer for Mommy?"

Sydney spoke to Harper in her tiny voice, "And we can ask Momma to give Pop-Pop and Nonna a feeling hug in heaven."

Charles helped the girls get down on their knees and knelt in between them as they bowed their heads to pray. When their prayer ended he gave each of the girls a kiss and a feeling hug, then he tucked them in under the covers.

Charles settled into a chair near Harper's bedside and watched over his daughters like a sentinel until they fell asleep.

Mourning Morning

A month had passed since Joelle's death but it seemed like only yesterday to Charles. He arranged the funeral service according to Joelle's wishes His five brothers and Rubin served as Joelle's pallbearers. The Duemijons were at the service, they helped with Harper and Sydney; everything else that happened over the month was a blur. Charles wished he had the power to turn back time.

Charles awakened from a beautiful dream to a horrific nightmare. His daily source of inspiration was snatched away. He was drained of all his strength. He longed for Joelle. He missed her so much it felt like splinters of broken glass were jammed into his heart.

His daughters were gifts from the love he shared with Joelle. His daughters were also reminders of the loss he would endure for the rest of his life. Joelle haunted him through the caramel colored complexions of their children. Their eyes, filled with her intelligence and curiosity, made him long for his best friend. He saw Joelle's smile on each of their daughter's bright faces. It was like Joelle's echo. The presence of Harper and Sydney was a reminder of Joelle's absence.

Charles was scared. It was not the first time he

faced fear but in the past he was always prepared. His father prepared him to be a man. The Marines prepared him to be a solider. He prepared himself to succeed in his business. He prepared for a blissful future with his wife and children. Today he faced a new fear. He was not prepared. How could he have ever been prepared for Joelle, ten years younger than he was, to die before him? How could he have prepared to raise two young girls without their mother? It was unfathomable the cornerstone of his foundation could be removed without any warning. The future seemed uncertain without Joelle in his life and it scared Charles everyday; but prepared or not he was going to face his fear.

Charles took Harper and Sydney early in the morning after breakfast with the Duemijons. It weighted on his heart taking the girls away from their grandparents while they were still grieving. The weight was multiplied by five when he told his brothers the girls were not available for the monthly dinner at his house. The family was devoted to his children but Charles needed time alone with his girls. Charles knew Joelle would have suggested a place where there was light and laughter so they could begin to heal. Charles knew the perfect place.

Rollercoasters

Harper was silent during the hour-long car ride from the city. Charles helped his girls out of the car when they arrived at their destination. Sydney held his hand tightly. Harper clung by his side but did not accept his hand.

Sydney broke free from his grasp as they approached the amusement park entrance. She danced in circles, wildly flinging her little arms up in the air. She ran back to Harper, purposely bumping up against her, she asked excitedly, "Harper, can we ride on the big roller-coaster together?"

Harper said, "Sure." She took Sydney's hand and pulled her through the entrance toward the ticket booth.

Charles allowed the girls to walk slightly ahead of him. Sydney screamed with excitement. "Daddy, come on, hurry up! We have to get ticsets to ride this one!" She pointed to a sign with the height requirements and ticket prices. Sydney was just above the line. Jumping for joy she shouted. "Yippeeeee, I *am* big enough now! See I told you, I told you!"

Charles caught up with Sydney in two strides and scooped her up while Harper waited patiently.

"Yes, Sydney you are *tall* enough to ride and I'm going to get three *tickets*," Charles said providing a new vocabulary word while also correcting Sydney's pronunciation. He was sure his efforts would have pleased their mother. He imagined Joelle smiling down on them and it made him feel better.

He hoisted Sydney up higher to swing her around. She squealed. "Yippeeeee!" then shouted happily, "Momma said the next time I would be big... ...*tall* enough and I am!" she said.

Charles worked through the sudden stab of pain he felt. It was not physical it was the visceral emotional memory of his last visit to the same amusement park. He remembered his family was whole, intact and unbroken back then. He shared a fun day with the love of his life and their two little girls. He shook the memory away. He was able to make his tone cheerful when he said, "Sydney you know your Mommy was always right!"

He felt Harper take hold of his hand. He looked down and Harper looked up at him. Harper's eyes were filled with understanding. She gave him an encouraging smile. It was the first time Charles saw Harper smile since her mother's passing. *'My little girl is growing up,'* he thought then he scooped up Harper. He jogged over to the ticket booth with both girls secured to his large frame. Sydney and Harper laughed as they held on tighter while he juggled them around and squeezed them to pull his wallet out of his pocket. He bought three tickets to ride the big rollercoaster.

Charles was not sure what kind of father he would become but he was committed to hang on with his daughters through every twist and turn until the ride was over.

Chapter Nine
H & S - New Unit

Single Father

The rollercoaster at the amusement park the day he took his girls alone was nothing compared to the ups, downs, twists and turns Charles experienced being a single father. Charles was in for the ride of his life. Literally and figuratively he rode on many more rollercoasters with Harper and Sydney.

Charles was thankful his in-laws and brothers were there to help pick up the slack when he needed it. He still questioned if he was capable of raising the girls properly without Joelle's guidance. He was building a strong family unit with his girls, yet there was still a hole in his heart. Every night he got down on knees with his children and prayed to God, their mother and her angels to help them make it through the next day. He exchanged *feeling* hugs with his children before he put them to bed. Then he spent a sleepless night on Joelle's side of the bed worrying about the long-term effects on his children without a mother in their lives. His worry was unnecessary. Harper and Sydney erased all of his doubts about being a good father. There were typical quarrels but no argument was ever serious. Charles was able to tune into their feelings and manage their mood swings too. He learned to communicate with his daughters and taught them better ways to communicate with each other. He most admired when Harper and Sydney supported and worked together, they were an excellent team.

Charles helped his little girls blossom into strong independent young women. They demonstrated they loved him and respected his opinion. They trusted him. They discussed their private thoughts and dreams. His daughters were comfortable talking to him about everything including the subjects Charles wanted to avoid like puberty and boys. During those sensitive discussions Charles perspired heavily but he did his best to advise Harper and Sydney in the way he thought Joelle would have wanted.

Harper & Sydney

Harper and Sydney were unique individuals who inherited the physical and character traits of their father and mother, Charles and Joelle Ellison. The Ellison Sisters looked alike but their personalities were polar opposites.

Harper preferred to be alone. She found happiness in arranging objects and putting them in their proper place. Harper was extremely articulate but she chose to speak only when it was necessary. Harper challenged Charles, always keeping him on his toes. She debated him regularly and won most of the debates. She simply stated the facts she researched to support her positions. Harper was curious about everything; like her mother Harper's mind was constantly calculating odds or thinking about possibilities and options. Harper was brilliant, she was a quick leaner and a superb problem solver. She excelled academically, math and the sciences were her favorite subjects.

Charles was confident assisting Harper with math, geometry, measurements and dimensions but he was out of his element when it came to the sciences. There was no need for Charles to worry because Harper was resourceful and capable of independent learning. She solicited the help of her Uncle Doctor Joe for her science studies. Harper was willing to share everything she learned. She voluntarily helped her sister with complicated science projects and taught her how to use the personal computer Charles bought for them. Charles was proud of Harper's self-motivation and initiative. He enjoyed watching the exchanges between his daughters. Sydney's math and science skills improved dramatically as a result of Harper's tutoring. Harper had an innate talent for teaching. Charles learned from Harper to; he became proficient with the personal computer.

Sydney was an extrovert, she was happiest around people. She talked non-stop, giggled and laughed loudly at the slightest things. Sydney and Harper shared a love for music but Sydney always turned up the volume. Sydney made a lot of welcomed noise in the house. She constantly shared her new creative ideas with the family. She was an artist. She spent her time painting the picturesque property or sketching portraits of her uncles. Sydney enjoyed working with her hands creating things. She asked Charles to buy her a hot glue gun; she was relentless. He finally gave in after she promised to follow his rules. Charles taught her how to use it properly and safely to ease his mind about purchasing a potentially dangerous tool for his young daughter. He made Sydney promise to use it only in the workshop he constructed outside their home.

Sydney was elated her father invited her to work in his *private workshop*. She spent most of her time in his workshop carefully using the hot glue gun in the way he instructed. She created a collection of eclectic brightly painted shadow-boxes and filled them with materials her father discarded. She customized some of the boxes for family and friends by adding things related to their individual personalities. She gave the customized boxes as gifts and sold the others. She was a talented entrepreneur.

Sydney used the money from her art sales to buy clothes. Art was her passion closely followed by clothes shopping and giving fashion tips. Harper had no fashion-sense so she valued Sydney's advice. Sydney helped Harper choose the right colored blouses to coordinate with skirts or pants and she made shoe suggestions to complete Harper's ensembles. Whenever Harper received compliments about her chic attire she gave Sydney all the credit. Sydney was a trendsetter. Charles refused to allow Sydney to buy anything he felt was inappropriate for her age; but it was not often he objected to her choices; and if he did Sydney negotiated until they came to a compromise. Sydney was confident in making her own decisions.

Uncle Brothers

Harper and Sydney learned they were a part of the Ellison legacy. They learned about PopPop-CharlesR and Nana CoraLee from their father and uncles. They learned about their history and all the branches of the Ellison family tree through scrapbooks, photographs and memorable oral stories. The Uncles entrusted the nieces to keep their grandmother's collection plus many other newer photo albums. There were pictures and clippings of old and new Ellison construction projects. There were many other family photo albums with pictures of their mother. Harper and Sydney cherished the collection and considered it an irreplaceable family heirloom. The sisters bought a large fire-safe to store everything then repurposed their grandmother's old cedar-wood chest to store their mother's wedding dress.

The Ellison Brothers took their roles as uncles very seriously. They provided protection for their nieces. No one could get close to Harper or Sydney without passing through the uncles. Harper and Sydney were fortunate to have their father plus five trusted men to turn to for guidance. Harper and Sydney looked forward to spending time with them. The Uncles with their unique views and different opinions left lasting impressions on the girls.

Uncle Byron explained human behavior and the impulses and desires of the mind. He encouraged his nieces to observe humanity and to ponder the universe. He was a practitioner of psychology and sociology. He was a good listener. He allowed Harper and Sydney to express their feelings openly without judgment or betrayal of their trust. Uncle Byron was the person they counted on for an objective opinion.

Uncle Doctor Joe taught them about the importance of good health habits. His advice was always about nutrition and exercise. He told them, "Start now and you'll make maintaining good health a lifestyle." He spoke Italian fluently and encouraged the girls to learn languages. Uncle Doctor Joe was also an exceptional swimmer. He taught both girls how to swim. Harper was a good swimmer but preferred other sports. Sydney was a little mermaid. Uncle Doctor Joe spent his limited free time outside his medical practice with Sydney in the pool or at the local beaches. Joe told Charles it was a needed mental health break spending time with Sydney. Sydney developed swimming and diving skills beyond Uncle Doctor Joe's capabilities. Sydney said she was going to be an artist and a lifeguard. She became a certified lifeguard with Uncle Doctor Joe's help.

Uncle Ron was a great coach for Harper. He taught Harper how to use her muscle memory, agility and strength. Harper enjoyed spending time on the basketball court with Uncle Ron. She was a good player with endurance. She learned how to dribble with both hands and to do crossovers in between her legs. Uncle Ron took her to the community center and on the polyurethane gym floor they played one on one, practiced free throws and ran defense drills. Harper took immense pleasure whenever Uncle Ron expressed his frustration at her fast break and maneuvers to the hoop before he could block her shot. Harper explained it was physics; he was taller but she was faster. Uncle Ron bragged, "You're still my little protégé."

Harper felt like she was Uncle Ron's protégé. They shared similar interest. Basketball was Uncle Ron's outlet but math was his world. Harper felt the same, she liked sports but she was passionate about math. Harper learned about measurements and geometrical configurations from her father but Uncle Ron introduced her to negatives, positives, profits, losses, interest, accruals and balance sheets. It was fun for Harper learning new terminology and working with numbers in a new way.

Uncle Ron promised he would teach Harper all about the company books including how payroll worked. He installed software on her new laptop. It was exciting because Harper understood it meant in the future she would learn about the financial management of the family business.

Uncle Gene traveled a lot performing. Music was his thing. He also spoke several languages and told funny jokes. He taught Harper and Sydney all about music and introduced them to different genres including classical, the blues and his personal favorite, jazz. Every time Uncle Gene visited he bought new records; and as technology progressed, he bought them a compact disc player and music CDs. He shared the music from all the countries he visited. Uncle Gene expected Harper and Sydney to give a critique of the music he shared. He wanted them to express how the music made them feel. He told them, "Music should affect emotion...if it stirs something in your soul then it has served its purpose...if it doesn't make you *feel* something then it's just a bunch of noise."

Harper and Sydney enjoyed Uncle Pauls's visits the most. He was their official Godfather. They remembered the days when Uncle Paul lived with them and ate a lot of buttered biscuits. When Uncle Paul came to visit he helped them build things with their father and he always had stories to tell. Harper and Sydney would listen attentively as Uncle Paul would begin telling a tale under the watchful eyes and keen ears of their father. If the story began to drift too far into adult themes their father would wag his finger at his younger brother and say, "Okay Bro that's enough." It was his way of censoring Uncle Paul. Harper and Sydney thought their father was keeping them from hearing all the juicy stuff because Uncle Paul's stories were about his street adventures and colorful characters. Apparently their father felt some parts of the stories were not appropriate material for little girls. Harper would express her disappointment and Sydney would beg her father to let Uncle Paul finish. Paul would look at his brother with apologetic puppy-dog-eyes and cut the story short.

After school and the busy days of activities with their father and uncles ended night would fall. Harper and Sydney would sit in the garden looking up at the stars spread across the sky. They search for the constellations while talking about memories of their mother. Harper and Sydney missed their mother the most at night.

While their father was sleeping restlessly during the night, Sydney would slip into Harper's bed and rest her head on her shoulder. It was Sydney's way of showing Harper she missed Mommy but was glad she had a sister. Harper would hold Sydney close and place her thumb briefly in her dimpled chin like a gentle kiss. It was Harper's way of showing Sydney she missed Mommy too but was glad she had a sister to help her through it. They squeezed each other tight to *feel their hugs* and console each other until sleep came and the morning light appeared. No one and nothing could ever come between Harper and Sydney.

Sisters Thick & Thin

Harper's hands were balled into fists ready to launch a barrage of pummeling blows on the older boy who shoved her little sister to the dirt in the schoolyard. She yelled at him. "Hey you knocked my sister down!"

The boy ran to the other side of the school yard and joined a group of boys playing football. He never looked back.

Harper's ears grew hot when she saw the dirty bloody scrapes on Sydney's knees. She brushed the dirt and gravel from her sister's dress. She was furious at the boy. He was too big and too old to be picking on little Sydney and it was not the first time.

Harper told Sydney after she completed a full inspection, "You're okay."

She helped Sydney get up from the ground. There was a distinct height difference between the sisters. Harper was thirteen and Sydney was eleven.

Sydney was happy. "Harper I think Natty likes me," she said as she brushed at a dirty spot Harper missed.

Harper was surprised and not sure she heard Sydney correctly. "What did you say?" Harper pointed to the bully playing with the other boys on the monkey bars.

He was swinging and jumping up and down for his friends. Harper thought he was also showing off for Sydney. Harper asked, "Do you know that boy?"

Sydney looked down at her bruised knees and soiled dress. She could tell Harper was mad but she could not suppress her smile. Sydney explained as if she were reading highlights on the boy's resume.

"His name is Natthaniel, not Nathaniel, Nath-tha-neil. Isn't that a nice name? His name has two T's and he has two dimples! He's in your grade. He's really good at sports,"

Harper stared at Sydney in disbelief.

Sydney pleaded, "Please don't beat him up Harper!"

Harper snatched Sydney's hand and pulled her along while she warily watched the boy named Nath-tha-neil.

After the schoolyard incident with Sydney, Harper began to notice Natthaniel Adams in her classes. He was a quiet student unlike the wild personality he displayed at recess. Harper met him in the hallway between classes. She told him to stop picking on her little sister, then she asked him a bunch of stuff so she could tell Sydney. She became curious about Natthaniel when he told her about his background. It was the first time Harper met someone with a parent from an island like her grandma Manuela. Once Harper figured out Natthaniel's taunting of Sydney was his way of trying to make friends she thought it was amusing.

Harper invited Natthaniel to her fourteenth birthday party. He came with his parents. Her father entertained Mr. and Ms. Adams. Harper played host to her party guests while Sydney gave Natty a tour around the house. Natty's favorite place was the kitchen. Natthaniel Adams and his family became great friends of Charles Ellison and over the years Natthaniel made himself at home in the Ellison's kitchen.

Chapter Ten
CHARLES - Notices & Deals

Missing

Charles established protocols for all visits and trips with his girls. It was the only way he could keep track of their busy schedules between school, extra curricular activities and everyday life events with his larger family.

He also decided to invest in a mobile phone. The cellular phone gave Charles peace of mind; as a busy single father the girls could reach him anytime. He could call home to check on Harper and Sydney and he could be reached in an emergency. All his brothers had mobile phones too. Ronald complained it was an expensive monthly expenditure. Charles said it was a necessity for the business to move into the future and change with the times. Charles thought the mobile phone was the best invention since the automobile. The phone did not work everywhere but he could call from any construction site in the city and if he was in nearby New York, New Jersey or Delaware he did not have the expense of long distance calls. Ronald appreciated those cost savings.

Charles used his mobile phone when he was out on his own property inspecting the grounds surrounding his home. He was continually expanding the house for his daughters. He was planning additional enhancements to the property including clearing more brush off the land to increase the size of the garden and adding a pool with a pool-house.

Charles called Joseph from his mobile phone to see if he took Sydney swimming.

Joseph was just finished with his last patient for the morning. "Perfect timing," he said. Charles asked already knowing the answer. "Joe, do you have Sydney?"

Joseph told Charles, "No, I have patients today. Sydney and I are scheduled for tomorrow."

Charles was in a panic, he told his brother, "I've searched the house and the entire property calling for her and she's no where in sight! I'm calling the police!"

Charles pushed the button on his mobile phone and disconnected Joseph. He ran back to the house to call the police on the house phone to report Sydney missing. The police officer took the information over the phone and when Charles gave her his address she asked, "Is this *the* Charles Ellison, the construction guy?"

"Yes," he confirmed. His heart was racing but his voice was steady as he made his report. "My daughter, Sydney Marie Ellison is missing. She was here on our property. She wouldn't leave the house on her own. I need someone here immediately. We need to find my daughter, she just turned twelve." There was a crack in his voice when he reported Sydney's age. Charles thought of Harper and immediately hung up on the police and called Paul's mobile phone. Charles felt his heart beating so hard and fast it felt like it was going to jump and run out of his chest. He was able to slow it down by the time Paul answered.

"Hey Bro, Harper's with you, right?"

"Yeah Bro you know it's my day on that crazy calendar you keep. What's up? You need me to bring her back home?" Paul knew something was wrong because Charles rarely disrupted his scheduled time with his nieces.

"Sydney is missing. She's not in the house or on the property. I've searched her hiding places and I know she wouldn't sneak off, it's not like her. I reported it to the police." Charles could not say anything else, his heart was racing again.

Paul told his brother, "We'll be right there. I'll call the brothers and I got some other people I'm gonna call."

Crossing the Line

Charles opened the front doors as Paul pulled into the driveway. Paul arrived at the house before the police drove up the access road. Paul could tell by his brother's facial expression Sydney was still missing. Charles pulled Harper into his arms and held her tight before he took her into the house. "Nothing yet," he said to Paul.

The police parked next to Paul's jeep. Paul stepped inside the house and stood behind Charles. The two police detectives approached the front door and showed their badges. "Mr. Ellison, you reported your daughter is missing. We're here to help. May we come in please?"

The detectives did not see Harper standing behind Charles. Harper was hidden by her father and uncle. She was listening and observing the entire scene. It was the first time she heard Sydney was missing. Harper asked, "Where's my sister?" Before anyone could answer she went running through the house calling out Sydney's name. "Sydney...Sydney...Sydney, where are you? Stop playing! Come out NOW! SYDNEY!"

Harper's voice traveled around the house as she ran to every room searching for her little sister. Charles was in turmoil seeing and hearing Harper's distress.

Paul touched his shoulder and told him, "Don't worry

Bro, I'll take care of her, you deal with the cops."

Charles ushered the police into the library and closed the pocket doors.

"I'm Detective Albert Wilson. I've been assigned to your case Mr. Ellison. This is Detective Clemmond. We understand the sensitivity of the situation, we'll handle this discreetly."

Charles shook hands and offered them a seat at a reading table. Detective Wilson sat down and pulled out a pen and a small notebook. Clemmond pulled out a large recording device from a carrying case and a smaller device. Clemmond went straight to the phone on the desk and started attaching the recording device.

Charles gave a detailed description of Sydney to Detective Wilson right down to the cleft in her chin. He took a picture out of his wallet and explained to the detective the last time he saw Sydney was in the garden. He said after their breakfast she went to paint. He went into his home office to make a business call. He told both officers,

"The security gates are not installed yet. My girls never go pass the access road. Sydney would never go down the road alone. Somebody came on the property and took my daughter. She didn't run away!"

The detective agreed. "I suspect you're right Mr. Ellison. Your family is well known and wealthy. It makes sense."

Charles displayed no emotion while the detective informed him of the standard procedures for child abductions.

"We'll need full access to the property to do a thorough search and check for any foul play or signs of a struggle."

The detectives exchanged a look between each other, it was a necessary procedure to rule out the parent's involvement before investigating other unknown subjects. Albert closed his notebook, stood up, opened the doors and walked out of the library. Charles and Detective Clemmond followed.

"Your property is huge. You still building on it?" Detective Wilson asked.

Charles ignored the detective's question because it was apparent he was expanding with construction equipment and supplies on the property.

Detective Wilson said, "I've never been in any of the Ellison Construction properties but I've heard they're all nice. Your home is very impressive."

Charles was loosing his patience. His tone was sharp

and direct. "You're welcome to a take full tour if it will help you find my daughter faster Detective."

Paul returned and reported Harper's condition to Charles. "She's upset. She's in Sydney's room. I told her you'd be up after you finish here."

Charles nodded his head as they walked back toward the library. "Thanks Paul."

Detective Wilson introduced himself to Paul then asked Charles, "Do you have another phone in the house?"

Charles pointed to the opposite end of the house. "There's a cordless in the kitchen."

The Detective was straight forward. "Whoever took your daughter wants something from you in return. The only way they're going to get it is to make contact."

Detective Wilson walked to the kitchen and retuned to the library with the cordless handset, it was fully charged. Clemmond took it and snapped it open. He placed something inside then snapped the set back into place and returned it to Wilson. Clemmond sat down at another reading desk with his monitoring equipment. He connected a headset, placed it over his head and adjusted the earpiece.

The two phones rang as if on queue. Charles sat

down at the library desk. He let the desk phone ring twice as instructed, then picked it up at the same time Detective Wilson answered the cordless phone. The detective pushed the cordless phone's mute button and shared the phone so Paul could hear the conversation. Clemmond was monitoring the recording equipment while listening.

The man's voice was muffled but Charles could hear his demands. "You'll git your daughter back if you do what I say. You understand?"

"Yes, I understand," Charles said with clenched teeth barely able to control his anger.

"Awwright den, you do what we say and der ain't gon be no problems. First, no cops. Second you ain't testifying in no federal case against the city and if dey call you say you ain't instrastid in buildin downtown no mo. Three, den you gotta send money... I'm gon give you three amounts and a account number. Write dis down."

Charles wrote down the amounts and an account number on his monogrammed stationary. The detective wrote the same information in his notebook.

"We git the money, den first thing tomorrow morning you git ya daughter."

The detectives continued to listen in on the call while Paul gestured he heard enough. He left the library and used Charles' private office to make calls from another phone line.

Charles was furious. There was no way in hell was he going to allow a kidnapper to keep his twelve-year old daughter overnight! The detective motioned for Charles to look up at his note book. His heart skipped a beat when he read '**PROOF OF LIFE**' written in big block letters.

Charles demanded. "I want to speak to my daughter now! Where is she? Put her on the phone."

The man laughed. "She right here man, she ain't' hurt or nothin."

'PROOF OF LIFE' 'PROOF OF LIFE' 'PROOF OF LIFE, those words shot through his heart. Charles raised his voice, it was so loud the detective moved the cordless phone away from his ear. His voice was an amplified bass, it reverberated around the room and bounced off the walls inside the soundproof library. The detective actually thought he saw the books on the shelf shake when Charles shouted. "I SAID PUT MY DAUGHTER ON THE PHONE NOW!"

The man on the phone seemed unaffected. "Awww... man...be cool... she right here... Sydney say hi to yo Daddy."

Charles heard the phone being passed around then Sydney said, "Hi Daddy."

Detective Wilson gave Charles an okay sign. Charles squeezed his eyes shut and imagined Sydney's sweet face with his identical dimple. Charles lowered his voice like the equalizer of an audio system adjusting the bass to the treble. He purposely made it sound as if he was speaking to Sydney under normal circumstances. "Hi Honey, you okay? Where are you?"

Sydney sounded sad. "I'm drawing pictures in my sketch book now but I don't like the way it smells here. They have a big kitchen with machines but they don't have any food. I'm ready to come home. I'm hungry. I wanted…"

Sydney did not get chance to say what she wanted because the phone was abruptly snatched away while she was still talking. There was a tense moment when everyone listening on the line heard a tussle and the phone drop. Charles strained to hear something, then he heard Sydney's voice. "You're rude. I was talking to my Daddy!"

There was a loud clap and Sydney began to cry. Charles knew it was the sound of the man slapping Sydney. Charles was enraged and hurt at the same time.

The man hit his daughter! The sound of Sydney crying in the background was breaking his heart. Unable to defend his child Charles felt helpless in the situation. He vowed when he caught the man who put his hands on his daughter he was going to make him hurt. It was the first time Charles felt he could actually take a life the way he was trained to do in the military.

Charles listened for any kind of background noises. He did not hear Sydney crying anymore. Detective Wilson motioned for Charles to wait. The man returned to the phone and with a menacing tone he said, "I can't stand smart-ass kids. She made me do dat. She wouldn't give me da phone."

Charles took a deep breath and for Sydney's sake he played along. "I'll take care of everything right away. How can I contact you?" Charles asked.

"We'll call you when the banks open first thing in the morning."

Charles demanded. "Let me speak to my daughter again!" He wanted to tell Sydney he was going to bring her home.

The call was disconnected.

Paul marched into the library in full marine mode. He posted a thumbs-up to Charles indicating he was ready.

He spoke in a low whisper to his brother while the detectives checked the recording.

"You know I love your girls like they're my own and as long as I'm breathing I'm not going to let nothing happen to them. These motherfuckers crossed a line so we going to push them back across it. We're going to show them if anyone enters Ellison territory and tries to take what's ours there's a high price to pay."

Charles gave Paul his full support to do whatever was necessary to bring Sydney home.

Detective Wilson gave orders over his hand-held two-way radio. There was no need to continue searching the Ellison property. He put the walkie-talkie down so he could ask questions while taking notes. Detective Wilson was aware even with a ransom demand most child abductions did not end well.

"Did you recognize the caller's voice? Do you know of anyone who might have access to your property or to your daughter? Can you think of anyone who might do something like this? Any lead you can think of will help."

Charles was silent, Paul answered for him. "We have some people in mind." Detective Wilson spoke to Charles. "Mr. Ellison, I can work with whomever you want, but it's crucial they take orders from me. No one is to take matters into their own hands. Vigilante justice is against the law." The detective closed his notebook.

"Uniformed officers will be stationed at your residence, one outside at the end of the access road and one inside the main house. We recorded the call and I ordered a reverse trace so we can get the origin of the call. Stay by the phone Mr. Ellison in case he calls back. Detective Clemmond and I will check things out with your bother. I can radio our progress."

Charles was silent, Paul spoke for him again. "Charles needs to check on Harper. If you're going to help let's go!"

Paul did not wait for the police to move. He gave Charles a fist bump and left on his mission. The detectives rushed out the house to catch up with Paul.

Paul's Mission

Paul recognized the voice on the phone the minute the man started talking. It was Sterling a homeless, druggie street hustler well known to the drug dealers and drug users. His bad english and the mole over his left eye made him easily identifiable; people called him 'Sty'. Paul knew Sty did small jobs to buy alcohol, drugs and cigarettes but he never thought he would take part in a kidnapping. Paul figured Sty owed somebody a lot of money and in his desperation took the job to clear his debt. Sty did not have enough smarts or balls to plan a kidnapping by himself. Paul was going to find out who was pulling Sty's strings, but first he was going to find out where Sty took Sydney so he could bring her home unharmed.

Paul Ellison, like his brother Ronald, was well connected in Philadelphia. It only took one call to the right person for Paul to track Sty down. His connect gave him information leading back to the neighborhood where Paul once ran with Rubin.

Paul ditched the detectives and his jeep by cutting through a tiny little-known one way side street. He experienced déjà vu walking through the back-alley-ways on foot, yet there were many definitive changes. The large affluent homes with attached garages were now private fraternity and sorority houses. The residential neighborhood was cut off by new university dormitory construction. The campus-housing was nearly completed. There were many places Sty could use as a hideout. Paul scouted the area. The lights were on in one fully constructed building. Paul crept around the back of the building to break in but the back door was already unlocked.

Sty and Sydney were on the first floor of the building. Paul found them easily. Sydney was in an empty cafeteria sitting at a table drawing in a sketch book with colored pencils. Sty was sitting in the student lounge next to the cafeteria watching the wide-screen television. Paul could see through the frosted glass panes separating the rooms Sty was alone.

Paul stealthy maneuvered his way into the student lounge undetected. Paul was fast and Sty was no match for Paul's speed, size or combat skills. Paul grabbed Sty from behind and dragged him out of Sydney's line of sight. He held him in a sleeper-choke-hold then let him go before he passed out.

Paul's voice was a low guttural growl in Sty's ear, "Who you working for Sty?"

Sty looked up after his head cleared and saw a giant choked him. The giant picked Sty up like a rag doll and slammed him against the floor. Sty was pinned down with the giant's huge hand on his chest. He thought the giant cracked his ribs. He began to whimper.

"Look man, dey gave me a address, told me to grab da girl, den call her daddy and say what dey said. I'm pose sta' hold her for twenty-four hours, den I git paid. I hadta sneak on da property and sleep in da damn bushes to git her."

Paul pressed down harder on Sty's sternum. The air in his lungs was forced out and for a second he could not breathe, it was worst than the choking.

"Who told you to grab the girl? Tell me and I'll let you keep breathing!" Paul said as he released the pressure.

Sty was fully cooperative. "I only know dude's first name… but his boss is payin'. Look Man I was just tryin to git a cut of da money." Sty tried to explain.

"Give me all the names you know." Paul said while he kept an eye out for Sydney. She was still sketching unaware of what was taking place. Paul pulled Sty up to his feet and he starting talking faster.

"My man is Freddie but he work for Mr. Reggie… dats Reginald MacClean. He's a big time city councilman."

Sty rubbed his throat and turned his neck back and forth, he massaged his bony ribs then offered an apology. "Look man it was a accident. I ain't mean to hit her…she wouldn't gimme me back da damn phone. I ain't good wit no kids."

Paul lost control when he heard Sty's confession about hitting Sydney. He wanted to rip off the ugly-ass mole over his eye, instead he punched him in his face. The blow was so hard it knocked out some of Sty's rotted teeth. Sty sank to the floor in pain and held his bleeding mouth. Paul hovered over him and showing no mercy, he yanked him up again and held him against the wall with one hand around his skinny throat. Sty was unable to make a sound but tears were streaming down his face. Paul's face was an angry mask as he leaned down and moved in closer.

"Motherfucker! You kidnapping and beating on little girls?" Paul said through clenched teeth. He continued choking Sty with one hand until he saw the look of terror in Sty's eyes, then Paul slowly released his grip. Sty cried and with his vocal-chords damaged he could only whisper. "Look Man you knocked my fuckin teef out!"

Paul shrugged his shoulders, mimicking Sty's voice he said. "Look man it was a accident. I ain't mean to hit you.

I aint good with assholes." He forced Sty back to the floor and threatened, "If you ever come near my family again you gonna lose more than your fucking teeth." Paul stood over Sty and pointed to the floor. "Stay down there and don't make a motherfucking move."

Sty held his mouth and sat still not moving a muscle. Paul left him on the floor to take Sydney home.

Arrested

Detective Wilson gunned his Buick down the Ellison estate access road to catch up with Paul. Clemmond rode shotgun. They were able to keep up with Paul through the city until he made an unexpected turn and they lost him. Detective Wilson circled the neighborhood. Clemmond spotted Paul's jeep in a tiny alley. It was parked lopsidedly straddling the pavement and the curb. Detective Wilson cruised the area slowly then parked at the dead end between the private houses and dormitories. Clemmond called in their location and they continued the search on foot.

Detective Wilson spotted Paul as he moved swiftly around one of the buildings. Clemmond pointed him out. "There he is," he said ready to chase. Detective Wilson held his partner back. "Wait Clem, I want to see what he's going to do first. I think he can handle himself." Detective Wilson knew Paul was a former marine.

They watched Paul slip inside the back of the building before resuming their approach. They pulled out their weapons when they reached the open back door. The detectives searched the first floor. Paul and Sydney were no where to be found. They did find a man on the floor holding his mouth with his teeth scattered around him.

The man looked pitiful. The detectives holstered their weapons. Detective Wilson shook his head when he said, "Messing with the Ellisons ...What the hell did you expect?"

Clemmond helped Sty to his feet. He read him his rights and placed handcuffs around his skinny wrist. Sty became belligerent when his hands were cuffed behind his back. His voice was a harsh rasp. "Look Man ya'll ain't even gon let me pick up my teef?" Clemmond asked Sty, "Where's the girl?" Before Sty could open his toothless mouth to answer, Detective Wilson said, "She's with her uncle on her way home."

Detective Wilson and Clemmond led Sty out the building in handcuffs. They left his teeth. The local news outlets were gathered at the dead-end when they exited. Cameras flashed as the detectives hurried to get their suspect into the back seat of the Buick.

Safe

Paul was carrying Sydney into the house while Detective Wilson spoke to Charles on the house phone. Paul handed Sydney over to his brother. Charles cried tears of gratitude.

"Mr. Ellison, your daughter is with your brother Paul. We've arrested the man who took her and we're on our way to the precinct. I'll contact you soon."

Charles thanked the detective. Paul took the phone and hung it up for Charles.

"Did...he?" Charles lowered his head; the thought of his daughter being sexually molested was too terrible to think of; he could not finish his question.

Paul assured him, "She okay, but..." Paul turned Sydney's face gently and showed her father the mark on her cheek. Charles gave Sydney two soft kisses on the bruise.

Paul was quick to speak. "You're home now Syd. I'm sorry about the bad man but he's gone and he can't hurt you no more." Sydney did not speak, she clung to her father. Paul gave Sydney her sketch book and pencils. "Here ya go." He was sincere when he said, "I took a look at your drawings, they're really nice. You're a good artist. You should come work with us." Paul winked.

Sydney giggled.

Paul told Charles, "Somebody tipped off the press, but I made sure they didn't see us when I got her out."

Charles did not know where Sydney was or how Paul *got her out*, but she was safe now in his arms. Charles held onto Sydney and she wrapped her arms around his neck and squeezed so he could feel it. Sydney's embrace was like a cozy blanket for Charles. He was grateful to God and Paul.

"Mind if I hang around for a while?" Paul asked.

Charles needed and wanted Paul's company. "Thanks Bro," he said.

Paul smiled at Sydney and told her, "I'm hungry and I bet you are too! I know there's something to eat in that big fridge. I'm gonna go see what I can heat up."

Sydney laughed at her uncle Paul because everyone knew he was not a good cook. Paul brushed her little dimple with his large thumb.

Charles held Sydney securely in his arms and headed upstairs. He kissed her other cheek and said, "Let's go tell Harper you're home."

The next morning Detective Wilson visited to make sure Sydney was okay and to ask Charles followup questions. After the detective saw Sydney occupied in the library with her sister and uncle, he followed Charles into his home office. Detective Wilson took a seat and Charles sat behind his desk.

"Mr. Ellison we tried our best to keep this all under wraps. Unfortunately the press monitors police emergency calls; it's their way to...you know...get ahead of a story. It's not illegal...and well... your emergency call was intercepted. Consequently with your family's notoriety the call was reported in the morning newspaper. It's a small article, however there is an old unrelated photograph of you and Sydney and recent pictures of the suspect's arrest and mug shot." Detective Wilson was straightforward with his advise.

"Your daughter's abduction is a matter of public record, you can't deny it, but do not respond to any inquiries. Let the public record speak for itself; it works in your favor. A man took your daughter for money; he was arrested right away and your daughter was returned home unharmed. Sterling Jones has a long history of priors and with these new more serious charges he's going away for a long time. Case closed as far as the public is concerned."

Charles was listening waiting for the conversation to turn to the private concerns. Detective Wilson was true to form when he changed the subject.

"Now about the ransom demands Mr. Ellison. Sterling Steven Jones, also known as Sty, does not have a bank account and we doubt if he knows anything about city contracts. We suspect he was working for someone… but he's clamped up tight…he won't talk…to us."

Charles shrugged his shoulders. "Detective, our business in this city has always been a challenge. We're no longer interested in building downtown anymore and it has nothing to do with a fool taking my daughter. Ellison Construction is going beyond this city's limits."

"Hmmm… well that's progress." Detective Wilson glanced around the well-furnished office then at Charles sitting comfortably behind his ornate desk. He asked. "Aren't you curious about who owned those accounts Mr. Ellison?"

Charles answered, "Detective Wilson, I'm just happy my little girl is home safe and you caught her abductor. Thank You."

Charles stood and extended his hand. Detective Wilson shook it for closure. "You're Welcome Mr. Ellison. I'm happy your daughter is safe too."

Charles escorted the detective out of his home.

On Notice

The Ellisons Brothers called a meeting. The situation needed to be handled promptly. Ronald had the floor.

"Reginald MacLean, city councilman; married, one stepchild, one mistress, lived in Dallas, Texas until he married and relocated. I focused on his move to Philly. His wife's connections got him the city job. I traced the contracts and the city bids we loss, MacLean's name is on every one of them. I pulled some strings to obtain his financial records. There are transactions going all the way back to the city bombing disaster and the neighborhood rebuild. I have all the transfer amounts, dates, account numbers, company and personal names; including one Renaldo Fuller who receives a generous monthly deposit transferred to his international account. Everything tracks with the amounts of the pay-outs and MacLean's scheme. The fool put everything under his own name and address. The Feds have the information and the evidence."

Gene was excited after Ron's report. "A criminal investigation is finally underway! It's about damn time, it's great news. Solid Bro."

Ronald continued, "It gets better. The Feds were

investigating the city's construction practices for a while, my sources tell me they have informants willing to testify."

Gene was offended. "The city tried to destroy us! It's got to be in the evidence they found but the Feds never contacted us!"

Charles said, "Someone must have assumed we were witnesses, why else would they take Sydney and demand for us not to testify for the Feds. The cash was not the real motivation just another opportunity."

Ronald was blunt. "ECC is a minority owned company, as far as the Feds are concerned we don't matter. The Feds contacted the *white companies* to gather enough evidence to convict."

Gene said with satisfaction, "Well at least we can sit back and watch the sparks fly."

Joseph was not satisfied. He warned his brother. "Sparks set fires. I'm worried about the connection to Sydney."

Paul was confident. "Trust me, that connection is not happening. Sty ain't gonna to talk because his debts are paid."

"Except the one he owes to society." Byron added.

Charles informed his bothers. "According to Detective Wilson a guilty man was arrested for a crime, he'll serve time, justice served and case closed."

Ronald put it to a vote. "We're in agreement, let the Feds do their job?"

Gene responded. "Cool, it should be over quick with all the evidence."

Charles could tell by Ron's expression things were already in motion. Ronald moved on without further commentary.

"Okay then for our next project all we need is a GO."

Charles was ready. "Make it happen! I've already told the girls they're going on a long overdue Caribbean vacation."

The business meeting was adjourned. Byron took a bite of one of Charles' famous stuffed hamburgers fresh off the grill. He rolled his eyes up to the heavens as he relished the delicious flavor.

Joseph asked Charles, "How is Sydney doing?"

Charles smiled. "Syd's great, it's like nothing happened. She's with Harper in the workshop. It's Top Secret stuff. I'm not allowed in."

Joseph laughed.

Byron devoured the rest of his burger in three bites. He wiped his mouth with a dinner napkin then folded it across his plate. "I'm going to see if I can get top secret clearance, it'll give us a chance to talk...if it's okay with you?"

Charles liked Byron's suggestion. "Good thinking, thanks Bro."

Joseph was still concerned. "We should take precautions before anything else happens."

Paul spoke with conviction. "Nothing else is going to happen cause the Ellisons have served notice."

Final Deal

City-hall was a bustle of activity as people moved around offices performing their normal daily duties. It was not a normal day for Reginald MacLean. He was locked in his office shredding evidence. Reginald was trying to destroy all the lists of developers and banks he had bought in on his shady deals. Files containing original purchase prices for lots and properties with falsified assessments were turned into shredded confetti.

Federal agents were gathering evidence for years to root out major corruption in one of the largest cities in the nation. Reginald didn't think the federal government was going make the connection to the Ellison girl's kidnapping. It was all for nothing anyway and it was his own fault for working with amateurs. Freddie and Sty fucked up the plan. Reginald had no money to show for all his effort. Freddie was hiding out somewhere and the police caught Sty. There was only a brief mention of the crime in the paper. There was nothing on the local or national news. It took influence, power and connections to control the cops and the media. Reginald knew the Ellisons handled the situation and the fact scared the hell out of him.

Reginald had no influence or power left in the city.

His phone calls to the associates he made rich went unanswered, he was a ghost to them, a marked man. Someone turned in evidence. Money laundering, bank fraud, racketeering, misappropriation of federal funds and tax evasion were under the federal government's jurisdiction. All of the city planning financials were called into question. The federal investigation had come to a head and indictments were coming. Reginald was being brought up on official charges. He was going down in disgrace after working so hard to create his new persona of the respected politician. It would be a shock to a lot of people he fooled including his wife and stepdaughter.

Reginald would be required to surrender to the federal authorities in the morning. His girlfriend in the district attorney's office gave him all the information he needed to make an escape. He actually thought he could leave the country and start all over again except his plan was illogical, he did not think it through fully. He was using the same accounts he used to move city pay-out money for his own personal expenses and savings. Any decent forensic financial analyst could follow his trail. He had fucked himself.

The Feds stepped in and seized his bank accounts including the one in the Cayman Islands his wife and mistress did not know about. The house and the investments he lived on were in his wife's name. His greed and corruption fueled by a life of lavish spending finally caught up with him. He had nothing left to liquidate.

Shredding the files was pointless but it felt like an act of control. Reginald knew there was no deal he could broker that would allow him to avoid prison for his crimes. The Federal Government had him on enough multiple counts to lock him up for years but there was no way he was going to be locked up again. Renaldo Fuller was locked up for identify theft and check fraud. Reginald MacLean kept Renaldo Fuller out of prison once he was paroled. It was their secret. Reginald was not going back to his secret past life.

Reginald answered the phone. He expected to hear his wife Lynette's nagging drunken voice asking why she was still not able to access their bank account. He was surprised it was a man's voice on the phone he did not recognize. The man's tone was cold and the message was blunt. "You made it personal MacLean. Turn yourself in to the Feds because if WE catch you the Feds won't."

Reginald slammed the phone down and backed away from it like it was a poisonous snake. He was out of options except one so Reginald MacLean brokered his final deal with the devil. He wrote separate notes for his wife and stepdaughter and left them on his desk. He put the gun under his chin and pulled the trigger. His body and blood splatter was on top of the shredded paper.

Successors

Charles was a wealthy man with properties and investments to keep his family financially secure long into the future; he wanted to protect the future for his daughters before he passed on to see Joelle again. He felt a sense of urgency to review and update his estate plan.

Harper's twenty-ninth birthday was approaching. It was time for Charles to share important information impacting her future including a full financial disclosure. There were business assets but there was also something set aside for each of his daughters when they turned thirty. Harper earned a good salary working for ECC but her trust was worth more than a life-time of salaries. Charles intended to transition Harper's trust fund to her control. It included a strong portfolio of investments and interest baring accounts, stocks, bonds, properties, land, insurance policies; personal bank accounts and good old-fashioned cash. Harper's net worth was in the millions. Sydney's trust was financially sound as well. Charles was placing Harper in charge of Sydney's trust fund. It was only for three years until Sydney turned thirty. It was a precautionary measure.

Charles trusted Harper's decision making. He could not have hired a more competent business partner than Harper. She held degrees in Architecture and Engineering; and after becoming the youngest winner of the IIAD's Gold Star Award, Harper was appointed lead architect of ECC. Harper's education, training and mentorship paid off and from the feedback Charles received she was performing an exemplary job.

The plan for Sydney to join the company was also underway. During her summer as an ECC intern, Sydney pitched some interior design ideas under a pseudonym. The designs stood out from all the rest included in the proposals. The Ellison Development team selected Sydney's design as the finalist without ever knowing she was Charles Ellison's daughter. Charles was proud of Sydney's talent and accomplishment.

Although the scheduling protocols were long gone and they did not have a wall calendar anymore, Charles kept tabs on his daughters. They were grown women with different social circles. Harper was involved in the architectural community, attending seminars and special programs. Charles was aware Harper's social life was active and she had many suitors but she never spoke of any special romantic relationships. Harper spent time outside the business supporting her mother's foundations, the HBCUs and planning and attending related charity events. Sydney was achieving success in the artist community while being pursued by one young man. Charles was keeping an eye on the young lawyer. It appeared serious, but there were complications with their relationship. Charles was not sure if the man was the best match for Sydney, he did not think it was going to last.

Charles successfully raised two smart, independent women ready and well prepared to thrive in the world. Charles kept his promise to his wife. He thought Joelle would have given him a good progress report, but he knew all along she was coaching him.

Charles focused on raising his children and building the family business and now, the girls were adults, ECC was ready for international expansion and his successors were ready to take over leadership.

Gene told Charles he was not getting any younger. He kept badgering him to get out and have fun. He said he earned the right to enjoy life. Harper invited him to events and Sydney wanted to introduce him to some *mature* women. He got a good laugh when she emphasized *mature*. Charles was finally considering reentering the social scene; he could never replace Joelle in his heart, but he was ready for companionship.

Chapter Eleven

CHARLES – Retirement & Reunion

Catalyst for Change

Sydney's abduction was a catalyst for change in Paul's life. It set Paul on a new path, a life-saving journey. Paul realized his purpose.

Sterling Jones deserved to be punished for taking Sydney, but the encounter with Sty shook Paul to his core. The anger Paul suppressed because of all the shit he went through traveled to his fist and smashed away at the world's face. He tried to strangle the beast that used, abused and oppressed him just for being a Black Man. Paul's last image of Sty was of him on the floor; his ashen complexion, and drug addicted, malnourished body of skin and bones shaking with his mouth a battered hole of missing and rotted teeth. It was a stark reminder of Paul's own escape from addiction. The only difference between Paul and Sty was someone cared enough to pull Paul away from his demons and out of his hell. Paul's family was patient with him and held him down until he was able to get his shit together.

Sty's condition was too familiar to Paul. There were plenty of Black men like Sty in the funhouses where Paul used to play. Paul knew what it was like to fiend for something without rational control. Sty was unaware of how close he came to loosing more than his teeth. Paul had thoughts of taking Sty's life while he was choking him. Paul was a capable, proven killer trained courtesy of the U. S. government. He had metals to honor his combat success. It scared him to realize he could have taken a human life because of his own anger. The war left Paul with more than physical scars. Paul thought he better do something more positive to channel his anger than punching another Black Man in the face and almost choking him to death.

He decided to discuss an idea with his brother Joseph. He started an outreach by returning to the old crackhouse he used to frequent. He called it the funhouse although with his new perspective he saw there was nothing funny about the whole scene. The residents were ambivalent when they saw him coming. Some remembered Paul using with them so he used it as the conversation starter. Paul gathered information from the addicts about what they wanted most; some only wanted more drugs, many wanted help. Those willing to accept his help were provided a safe place with a good meal and time to eat, sit and talk. Paul was not surprised to find there were a lot of homeless and disabled veterans in the mix; it gave him another idea.

Soliciting volunteers from fellow veterans he met

through his sobriety and with a combination of support from his business connections and brothers, Paul set up an assistance program to help the veterans in the group gain access to entitled support services.

Paul worked one on one and in group sessions with the Vets who suffered from addiction. He was still an addict too but Paul was fifteen years sober and committed to his sobriety; he was a sponsor for those who were fighting their own private wars.

Helping Charles raise Harper and Sydney helped Paul saved his humanity. Helping the Vets saved his soul. Paul built a non-profit center; he thought of it, created it and nurtured it. It was a labor of love and it was Paul's baby.

The Mansa Center for Rehabilitation and Veteran's Services improved Paul's life. He established a foundation to fund it and the Mansa Center's reputation of service and authenticity became another Ellison success story. Dr. Joseph Ellison was a an advisor at the start, later he volunteered to assist with physicals and health screenings. Dr. Byron Ellison contributed too. He spent time at the center performing mental health checks and recommending specific therapies for those who needed care. Ronald kept track of the foundations's finances including its non-profit status, donations and expenses.

Gene was busy scouting for talent at the center. He set up entertaining events for fund raisers. Charles hired graduates of the foundation's construction program based on Paul's recommendations. The construction program graduates discussed in group sessions how physical work at ECC was therapeutic. It reminded Paul of his recovery time with Rubin. Paul had not seen his friend in a while. He decided to pay a visit to Rubin's to see if he might be interested in Mansa Foundation activities.

Family Offer

"Come on Rubin let us in—we don't wanna take this gate off the hinges. You know we can." Paul showed his toolbox to Rubin through the front door window. Rubin was not threatened by Paul or Charles. Rubin rolled his eyes, as if they were too heavy to move, the whites were slightly yellow. His faced was unwashed and there were small yellow-white spots of mucus in the corners of his eyes. His complexion was pale against his dark hair grown past his shoulders, a few long gray strands stood out prominently from all the rest. His unkempt beard was threaded with the same unruly gray hairs. Rubin peeped through the front door window and scratched his hairy chest. "What ya'll want? Shiiiit! I ain't feeling up to no company."

Paul knew Rubin better than anyone, he sensed his friend was in trouble. Rubin was thinner than when Paul last saw him. Paul was determined to get inside Rubin's house. Charles could see Paul was anxious to check out Rubin's situation. He tapped Paul's shoulder to let him do the talking. Charles reminded Rubin. "We're not company Bro. We're family so open up the door."

Paul was persistent. "Come on Bro. We came to see you. What's up?"

Rubin opened his front door but he did not unlock the outer gate. The key to the heavy duty lock was in his hand. He started to rant. "I did a good job for them motherfuckers, after they dragged my ass in there, cut off all my hair and tried to beat me down. But they ain't know I was good with my hands. Shiiiit I shocked them motherfuckers when I fixed their fucked up equipment and I straightened out all their shit while they slaved my ass out. Then they dangled that carrot Man, offered me more money and more rank. What I do...reenlist like a damn fool...trying to suck up all that mechanical training til they sent my ass back to Nam to airlift some of their asses out with those refugees! Shiiit, we recovered tanks too cause I fixed those bitches! Now when I'm done my fucking time and I need a job motherfuckers fucking with me. I showed my ID and they looked at my last name and they're were like... are you a U. S. citizen? Motherfucker! You sittin' comfortable behind a desk while I fucking fought for your white-collar-ass. My veteran status is all you fuckin' need...Shiiiit you questioning my name?... Motherfuckers!"

Rubin was on a tirade, rambling about the system; his denial of benefits and his last name. Suddenly he put the gate key back in his pocket and asked them, "Shiiiit why ya'll' over here fucking with me today?"

Paul pleaded, "Yo Rubin, hold on Bro. We ain't here to fuck with you. I got something important to talk to you about." Paul exchanged a look with Charles. Rubin waited with his eyes fixed on the two big men on his front porch.

Paul asked Rubin, "How would you like to get everything you're entitled to out of the system that's trying to fuck you?"

"Shiiiit now you talking Bro!" Rubin pulled the key back out of his pocket and unlocked the iron gate. He let Paul in first. Paul could smell the stench of urine coming from Rubin's clothes. Charles followed inside while Rubin pulled the gate closed; he did not lock it back but he closed his front door.

Rubin's house was a work of outstanding of colonial architecture with high ceilings, original wood moldings, ornate marble mantles and mosaic tile around the fireplace. Paul was happy to see the house was in excellent shape and the restoration workmanship from years prior held up well. Unfortunately Rubin's house was a mess. Multiple stacks of old newspapers were pushed up against the walls. A clutter of discarded bottle tops, old empty soda bottles and beer cans were piled in a corner near his back door. Rubin's clothes were ironed neatly and hanging on a pole attached to a rolling clothes-stand in the middle of the dinning room. The dinning room table was covered with clean clothes waiting to be folded.

"Imma go to the bafroom and wash up now since I got *family* here." Rubin said sarcastically.

Rubin left the room and the brothers seized the opportunity to look around and talk amongst themselves. The kitchen was surprisingly neat. All dishes were clean and stored orderly on the open shelves. There was no sign of any used pots or pans and the stove was spotless. Paul checked to see what kind of provisions were in the fridge. It was empty. He checked the pantry cabinet it was empty too. Paul looked at Charles with worry on his face. They spoke in low voices.

Charles asked, "You think you can get him to

accept our help?"

"I don't know but I'm gonna get him to talk to Byron." Paul said.

Charles was skeptical. "Rubin...talk to a therapist? Good luck."

Paul whispered. "I have an idea. Offer him a job."

Charles thought it was the perfect solution.

"What y'all doing snooping around in my kitchen?" Rubin returned from the bathroom and he looked much better. His face was washed and put on a clean undershirt and pressed jeans. The urine smell was gone. Rubin sat down at the dining room table and pushed aside the pile of clean unfolded clothes. He waited for Paul and Charles to come out of his kitchen. Charles sat at the dining room table with Rubin while Paul stood in the high archway between the two rooms.

Rubin asked, "So Paulie, how can I fuck the system?"

Paul said, "Before we fuck the system we could really use your help."

Charles followed Paul's lead choosing his words carefully. "Rubin we'd like to offer you a position at the company. We'll help you through the application process. All ECC employees get a check up before they start. It's a standard clearance procedure. The exams are private, we'll have Joe and Byron take care of you personally to speed up the process." Charles was proud his two brothers were well respected doctors in their fields. Rubin was looking at Charles waiting for him to get to the point. Charles cleared his throat and continued. "I'm offering you a position because we know about your skills and training. You would be able to hit the ground running. You would be an asset to ECC not to mention we trust you, because you're family."

Paul nodded and Charles finished. "Think about it Rubin but I need an answer soon because I'm stretched thin especially with Paul's foundation expanding. Joe and Byron are splitting their time between ECC and the Mansa Center so we'll schedule your appointments."

Paul picked up where Charles left off. He told Rubin about Mansa's nonprofit status, its mission and how they were fucking the system everyday.

Rubin thought it all sounded good and just in

time. He had a suspicion someone told the Ellison brothers he was broke after paying off his high property taxes. It was not a coincidence they showed up at his door unannounced. Paul and Charles were there to help him. He needed a job and he was definitely interested in volunteering for Paul's non-profit. They really were his family.

"So Bro, you coming in with us?" Paul asked.

Rubin answered, "Shiiit yeah I'm in." He stood and exchanged the marine handshake with his brothers from another mother then he sat back down and asked Paul, "Have you talked to Rita?"

Paul was unable to look Rubin in the eye but he was honest when he said, "We don't talk no more. We're different people now Bro."

Rubin started to fold the clothes on the table. "Shiiit, we all different now Bro," he said.

Crew Chief

Rubin liked to joke Paul suckered him in to the job, but it seemed it was his destiny all along. Rubin considered Paul his best friend and the Ellison Brothers treated him like family. Rubin was proud to be a part of the Ellison family and an employee of Ellison Construction Company.

Rubin accepted a position as a Construction Crew Chief. The Samson was his fourth project. He was in charge of every construction crew member on the site and their assignments. It was an easy job compared to serving in the marines.

Charles and Paul made a concerted effort to recruit from Black, Latino and Vietnamese communities. The crew was diverse. ECC was known as a good employer with a reputation fair pay and treating employees with respect.

Rubin spoke three languages. He was a great crew chief and an excellent machinist; he could fix anything needing mechanical repair including construction equipment, power tools and cars. The crew marveled at his skills.

Charles was an excellent boss, Rubin recognized great leadership. Paul was a good mentor for Rubin. Restoring Rubin's old house years earlier turned out to be Rubin's early training. Rubin settled in nicely with his new duties.

Rubin's hair was trimmed, but it was still long enough to be pulled into a ponytail under his hard hat. No one teased him about his hair; on the contrary, Rubin received compliments from women his age because most men his age were losing their hair.

Rubin stayed focused on the job. He checked the orders of the day. They were still ahead of schedule and ready for the site visit. Charles and Paul would be arriving soon. Rubin gathered the small crew together that gutted the building and prepared it for demolition. He applauded to show his appreciation for their hard work, then he made announcements. "You all did a solid job. Everything is ready. The CEO and COO are on their way, so after ya'll do the meet and greet stuff y'all can take tomorrow off." He repeated his announcement in Spanish and Vietnamese. The crew cheered and applauded about receiving a full-day off with pay.

Rubin was happy Charles and Paul Ellison were involved in day to day operations. They were in constant communication. It made Rubin's job run smoothly. A site visit from the top brass sent a positive message to his crew.

Site Visit

Paul was content with his life and comfortable in his own skin again. He split his time between the foundation, working with the Vets and visiting his nieces. He liked checking in with Harper and Sydney to see how they were doing and to get a preview of their new and interesting designs. Things were slowing down for Paul when it came to the construction business, he was still involved with ECC on a limited basis but he told Charles it was time to let the young ones take over.

ECC scheduled standard site inspections before and after each phase of a project. Charles considered it a requirement to maintain engagement and oversight. Paul looked forward to the site visits.

Paul drove while Charles looked out the passenger window at the evolving city skyline. It took years of hard work but they achieved one of their key goals. ECC was now also a part of the city's new and improved center city corridor. ECC was a big player in the construction industry, nationally recognized and gaining momentum on the international front. They employed engineers, architects, builders, plumbers and electricians. There were over fifteen hundred ECC employees.

Paul guided his new four-wheel drive sport utility vehicle through center city traffic and around the construction site. Paul told Charles, "Rubin said they're ahead of schedule."

"It'll be good to see Rubin and the crew again." Charles said.

"Yeah Bro, I'm glad he's in charge here, it gives you more downtime." Paul winked but Charles was still looking out the window. Paul asked, "Speaking of downtime, you got time to grab something to eat after we're done so we can talk about your birthday and this retirement party?"

Charles turned his attention to Paul. "Sounds like a plan, remember you're not far behind me Bro. There's a new soul food place Byron told me about...wanna try it?"

Paul was encouraged by Charles's suggestion. "Yo, Bro! You know if Byron recommended it, the food's gotta be good." The brothers laughed thinking about Byron's love of good food.

Paul parked next to a mobile trailer, it was Rubin's on site office. He cut the engine and pulled two hard hats from the back seat. Charles took one but before they got out of the vehicle Paul spoke with enthusiasm. "Bro, you always said we would get through all the bull shit and our business would be successful. Look at us now. We're downtown Bro!"

Charles spoke with sincerity. "I want you to know how proud I am of *you*, Bro. … with everything you did for the business…the things you're doing down at the center…what you did for Sydney, everything you do…for the girls…the family…me…and the things you've overcome to become the man you are today…you are an example of what Pop and Mom tried to teach us." Charles touched Paul's shoulder and finished. "To be honest I've always looked up to you."

Paul was humbled but it felt good to hear how his brother really felt about his efforts to make the family proud. They stepped out of the car and Paul gave Charles a strong bear hug. "I love you Chay." Paul said then playfully punched at Charles and joked, "I guess if I had your dimpled chin I'd be perfect." Charles laughed with Paul as they walked into the building to meet Rubin.

Accident

Rubin yelled for help but he was not going to get it. Paul was laid out on the side of the scaffolding with his leg twisted at an odd angle.

Rubin turned his attention back to Charles. He could see Charles was in a bad way. A thick wooden beam pinned him down on the concrete floor. He was conscious, but his hard hat was off and blood covered his face. Rubin took action. He lifted the heavy beam to free Charles and after he moved it he felt something in his arm pop. He yelled, "Shiiiit!…Shiiiit!…Shiiiit!"

Charles was free but he was not moving. Rubin found his hard hat and put it back on his head with his good arm, then he left Charles to help Paul.

Paul used Rubin's support to raise up on his uninjured leg and drag himself over to Charles. He gave a thumbs up to Rubin after they settled on the floor. Paul positioned himself closer to his brother despite the excruciating pain he felt in his leg.

Charles was confused. "What happened?" Paul told him, "The fucking building collapsed on us!" Rubin warned Charles. "Don't move! I think you hit your head." Charles ignored Rubin and tried to sit up to see the damage. He broke out in a sweat from his efforts but he was not moving. "It's not my...head I think it's my legs....I can't move them." Charles passed out.

There was a grinding sound and a loud bang outside then the entire building structure started to sway. Paul and Rubin used their bodies to shield Charles while a hail of bricks, twisted metal and falling debris came down on them.

Retirement

Ronald, Byron and Gene were at the hospital listening to Rubin describe the accident. Paul was in stable condition but sedated. They were still waiting anxiously to hear news about Charles. Harper was with Joseph and the doctors discussing his condition.

Rubin's injuries were minor compared to Charles and Paul. His arm was in a cast and sling. Byron put his arm around Rubin's shoulder carefully to comfort him. Rubin told the men who were like his brothers as much as he could remember. His eyes were full of regret and sorrow.

"We let the crew go home. We was talking then … I heard a bang outside…there was a rumbling noise all around us. Shiiiit I thought we were going to be crushed…the crane musta' crashed against the building."

Rubin could not think of anything else to cause the wall to collapse, but no matter the cause, it was still his responsibility to make sure the site was safe. He felt like it was his fault his brothers were hurt. Rubin said he failed Charles and Paul.

Ronalds's analytical mind reconstructed the

accident based on Rubin's story. Ronald spoke softly as if he read Rubin's thoughts. "Rubin it wasn't your fault. We know how thorough you are. We'll have someone investigate."

Byron chimed in, "Let's focus on healing the family and that includes you."

Gene spoke optimistically, "Yeah Man, it's going to be okay."

Rubin had an ominous premonition it would never be okay again.

Paul's feet were no longer his only bothersome medical issue. The surgeon saved his leg with titanium pins. He would need to use a cane for the rest of his life but at least he would walk again. Joseph helped Paul through months of physical therapy and they managed his pain without narcotics or opioids. His accomplishment was bitter sweet. He would have gladly given up his limb for a different outcome. Every time Paul's leg ached him he remembered the accident and his irreplaceable loss.

Charles did not recover, his heart stopped during the surgery to repair his spine. There was no attempt to resuscitate him, his DNR order was honored. The retirement party the Ellisons planned for Charles became his funeral.

Strong Will

Charles Randolph Ellison Jr.'s last wishes appointed his brother Paul Mansa Ellison as the executor of his estate. The first two lines of his Will read:

"If you are reading this I have officially retired from ECC and have hopefully rejoined my wife on an eternal vacation. It is up to another Ellison to pick up the hammer."

Harper and Sydney were consults on decisions about his personal belongings; wisely Charles declared Paul would be the tie-breaker if required. His daughters were financially secure with trust funds, company investments, properties, his life insurance and inheritance. Charles never spent money frivolously. He invested his money and with Ronald's advice he multiplied his investments. The Ellison Brothers inherited some of Charles' company stock. Charles made sure all the Ellisons would be connected through his explicit wishes.

It was not a surprise to the Ellisons that Charles left Rubin a small fortune. It was a surprise to Rubin who tried to refuse his inheritance. Paul would have none of it; he reminded Rubin the accident was not his fault and Charles loved him like brother. Charles also donated a substantial part of his fortune to the Mansa Center, the ManDane Library and the Duemijon School. Through established family foundations, Charles left endowments and scholarships worth millions to HBCUs and other educational institutions. There were specific requirements with provisions as to how the funds were annually distributed. In his final act of kindness, Charles left a renovated beach house in New Jersey to Mrs. Dunbar. It was a point of levity when they read it was to be used when she decided to retire. Mrs. Dunbar was well into her eighties and she had no intention of retiring but she would use the house as a summer vacation home for foster families.

Harper and Sydney planned a family dinner at the house after the reading of the will. It was Byron's suggestion to discuss the funeral arrangements over the dinner and before the meal was finished things were settled. The Uncles agreed to continue the tradition of monthly dinners at the house with Harper and Sydney. The Ellison dinners would honor Charles and Joelle and remind them all how important family was over everything else.

The Ellisons moved forward with the funeral plans. A public statement was released. Gene handled all press and business communications. The ECC Board Meeting would be convened within thirty days to announce the official succession plan. Ellison Construction Company employees would be notified before the public as Charles instructed.

Charles died at sixty-four. Harper was thirty-one and Sydney was twenty-eight. Harper and Sydney were always prepared for their father's death. Charles started preparing them right after their mother died. He was older than their mother and wanted them to understand one day it was bound to happen. They did not think about it on a daily basis. Death was just something they knew would eventually happen and when it came they knew they would be prepared.

Harper and Sydney held each other closely as they reviewed the details of their father's last wishes. Everything was arranged, there was nothing to do except follow his instructions.

"Just like him" Harper said.

"Yup, Dad always prepared for everything," Sydney said while she flipped through the funeral service program.

"I know, but it seems surreal he's not here." Harper

paced around her father's home office.

Sydney confessed, "I keep hearing his voice."

Harper confessed, "And I keep wanting to touch his chin."

Sydney told her,. "You know you can touch my chin anytime Harper."

Harper opened her arms. "I think we'll be all right Sydney, but I'm going to miss him." Sydney gave Harper a squeeze and Harper returned it with a hug Sydney could feel. Sydney told her sister, "I'm going to miss him too."

Harper and Sydney were women of faith, they believed their father was resting in heaven with their mother, but it was hard not having his presence after his death. There were many reminders he was no longer in the physical world. Harper missed the sound of her father's heavy footsteps in the house. Sydney missed the sound of her father humming with his power tools in the workshop whenever he was concentrating. There were other little things, like the extra height of the kitchen cabinets and his favorite coffee cup sitting next to their mother's tea cup on the shelf.

The Ellison Sisters were methodical with the sorting

of their father's personal items. They laughed and cried over the memorabilia. They packed away the things they knew their uncles would want; then cleaned out all of the things their father would have wanted donated to shelters and charity organizations. The house felt empty without their father's belongings filling it. They watched a truck drive away with the last of the boxes, Sydney proposed an idea. "After all this is over, let's go on a getaway just the two of us." Harper said, "Yes, we'll need a recharge to continue what he started."

Home Going

There was standing room only inside the church at the funeral services for Charles Randolph Ellison Jr.; outside, police cars barricaded both ends of the street from traffic. Foot-patrol officers ensured the news media and onlookers remained a respectable distance from the church steps to keep them cleared for the family to exit at the conclusion of the funeral service.

In spite of the heat, people stood shoulder to shoulder up and down the normally busy two-way street. It was the kind of summer day when the black-top on the streets shimmered from the hot sun and women fan themselves with whatever was handy. Naturals, weaves, curls and locks began to give in to the humidity. The crowd waited to say goodbye to a hometown hero. There were all kinds of people in the crowd; some knew or interacted with Charles Jr. and knew him as Chay; they were there to celebrate a life-time of shared memories. Some people were there for the spectacle of seeing the rich and famous Ellison family. Gangsters and wanna-be-gangsters stood far from the church and outside the police perimeter. Anonymity was a crucial requirement for a G's survival. They stood on corners swaying against the hot breeze, smoking cigarettes and an occasional joint while waiting to pay their respects to the Ellisons.

A carriage with six black horses stood outside the church entrance. Traffic noise punctuated by the chatter among the crowd had no effect on them. The horses' eyes were shielded from distraction by polished leather blinders adorned with brass fasteners and black feathers.

The church doors opened and the Funeral Director, a short and sullen man with white gloves exited. He gave instructions to the six pallbearers to lift the casket from the carrier and carry it in a slow and traditional march down the church steps. The American flag was draped and secured on the coffin's beveled top. A wreath made of red roses and baby's breath in the shape of a cross was carried in front of the casket by one of the clergymen. The six pallbearers turned in unison and placed the pearl white casket into the ornate carriage. The horses shifted on their muscular legs as they adjusted to the weight of their cargo. Miniature lights outside the carriage cabin glowed to life and burned bright, a signal the carriage was occupied.

The rest of the Ellison family began filed out of the sanctuary and entered the awaiting limousines behind the horse-drawn carriage. The rest of the mourners followed out;. they went to their parked cars; started the engines; turned on headlights and caution signals; placed bright orange funeral signs in the front windows; and formed a line behind the two leading limousines.

The barriers were removed by the policemen. A squad car cleared a path at one end of the long street. It moved slowly with red, blue and yellow blinking flashers and an occasion 'whoop-whoop' of the siren.

The Funeral Director took command and with a slow motion salute he climbed atop the carriage. He tipped his top hat to the driver and the driver tipped his top hat in return then tugged at the reins. The six horses obeyed his command and pulled the carriage into the street. The crowd gave the caravan a wide berth as the limousines and numerous cars joined the long procession. There were so many cars in the slow moving caravan the traffic-light changed a few times while vehicles crossed the intersection to follow the family to the cemetery.

The street crowd began to disperse, whispered voices returned to normal tones as folks expressed their emotions about the funeral. The printed program for the Home Going Service of Charles Randolph Ellison Jr. was an 8x10 booklet. It described his life history and contributions. There were color photos of the Ellison family and a list of the surviving family members. The glossy printed program was a prized possession.

Another Promise

Paul walked out the crowded church with Harper and Sydney by his side. The chauffeur assisted the three of them into one of the roomy limousines. Joseph, Ronald, Byron, Gene and Rubin were in a separate limo. A throng of press waited outside with cameras ready. They took photos and were respectful enough not to shout but they looked hungry and ready to pounce if given the opportunity for a sound-bite.

Paul knew the family would support Harper and Sydney but it did nothing to change the fact they loss their mother and their father much too soon. Paul was feeling what Charles experienced after Joelle's death. It weighed on Paul's heart he was spared and Charles was taken away from his daughters. Paul thought it was not fair because Charles was a father and Paul had no children. The familiar feeling of survivor's guilt took over Paul's emotions as he rode to the cemetery.

Today at his eldest brother's funeral Paul experienced a new level of anxiety about the future. He struggled with a new reality. Living with his addiction was not as scary to him as living without Charles. He was not trained for the situation. He had no weapons. He was vulnerable, unprepared and unprotected. Today he faced his anxiety and worry alone. How could he have prepared for the foundation of the family to be shaken to its core? How could he continue to maintain the business they established without his brother at the helm? These thoughts frightened Paul.

It was hard for Paul to take when Charles died. It changed everything. Paul's big brother was his main inspiration. There was a vacant space in Paul's heart with Charles gone. His brother's daughters temporarily filled the hole. The grace, beauty and strength of his nieces were reminders of Charles and Joelle. Harper's smile reminded Paul of the sister he never expected who loved and supported him when he needed it the most. The cleft in Sydney's chin was a reminder his big brother was always present. Harper and Sydney were part of the Ellison legacy and Paul would do everything to protect them. He remembered what he told Charles when Harper and Sydney were children. *"You know I love your girls like they're my own and as long as I'm breathing I'm not going to let nothing happen to them."*

Paul was still breathing and he was going to keep the promise he made to his brother.

Reunited

The Ellison Sisters sat quietly holding hands at the gravesite and said a final goodbye to their father. They were surrounded by uncles, extended family and close friends. There was no press. Joseph, Ronald, Byron and Gene, served as pallbearers; Natthaniel and Dean volunteered to stand in for Paul and Rubin. The Ellison Brothers, took their places behind Harper and Sydney. The pastor prayed over the coffin; marines fired three volleys into the air with their rifles followed by the traditional military taps Gene played on his trumpet. It was the final call for Charles Jr.. Four marines in full dress-blues removed the American flag covering the coffin and performed the ceremonious flag folding. One marine handed Harper the tightly folded triangular shaped flag. Harper accepted it on behalf of the entire Ellison family. The marine stood at attention then presented a slow-motion salute to the family, when the salute was completed he did an about-face turn and marched to his station along side the other marines. The bright blood stripe on their uniforms was visible as they turned and marched in synchronization out of the cemetery.

Charles Randolph Ellison II was laid to rest next

to his beloved wife Joelle Duemijon-Ellison. Harper and Sydney experienced unimaginable loss yet they were comforted by the belief their father and mother were finally reunited. It was a solemn moment but the Ellison Sisters held their heads up high.

Excavation

The Ellison Brothers gathered after the burial to talk about the report Ronald received from the private investigators. Ronald showed everyone a thick report full of structural photos, contracts, documented interviews and written narratives. Paul listened with Joseph, Byron and Gene while Ronald shared everything in the report. When he was finished, Ronald directed his question to Paul, "How do you want to handle this?"

Paul said, "That motherfucker! I knew it! That explains why our engineers said the building's foundation was weak. We don't build weak shit!" His brothers nodded their heads in agreement. Paul looked at his brothers and took command. "Chay would have wanted us to act fast." Paul asked Ron, "What was the name of the excavation subcontractor?"

Towers Part 1 - Foundation

Chapter Twelve
H & S - Knight Shifts

White Knight

Dean Delgado earned the respect of Sydney's father and uncles. The Ellisons seemed to accept him and his Italian heritage. Feeling confident enough to seek Mr. Ellison's approval to marry his daughter, Dean bought an engagement ring and spent a week preparing one of his best opening arguments to present his case. As fate would have it, Dean's proposal was put on hold and instead of driving to the Ellison estate to seek Mr. Ellison's approval for his marriage proposal, Dean drove Sydney to the estate to pick out a suit for her father to wear in his casket.

Mr. Rubin was still recovering from the accident. Dean volunteered to replace Mr. Rubin as a pallbearer. It was something honorable Dean thought he could do for Mr. Ellison. Dean completed the solemn duty of carrying the heavy casket with four of the Ellison Brothers and Natthaniel Adams. Then he stood behind Sydney Ellison and other family members seated around the gravesite.

Dean touched Sydney's shoulder when her father's coffin was lowered into the ground. Sydney touched Dean's hand to show her gratitude for his support.

Dean gave Sydney time to grieve after Mr. Ellison's death, but he stayed close to her over the months. Finally, when he thought she was ready, Dean surprised Sydney with the ring and marriage proposal. He told Sydney he wanted to move out of his apartment to a place closer to her until they decided where they would live together. Sydney asked him not to move and to keep their engagement a secret.

Black Knight

Harper loved her home but it was too quiet without her father. Once, when Uncle Paul stopped by unannounced, she hurried to the foyer thinking her father was home and everything after the accident was a bad dream. It was not a bad dream. Her father was never coming home again. It was her reality.

Harper collected the sympathy cards spread throughout the living-room of the estate. She packed them in a large box to send the family's acknowledgments later. She took a quick look around the room. There were flowers everywhere, more condolences for their loss. Harper planned to donate all the flowers to the hospital except the personal arrangement of yellow roses she received from a friend.

Natthaniel asked, "Is that it?"

Harper gathered up the yellow roses, "Yes, that's all, thanks Nate."

Natthaniel picked up the box of cards and grabbed the handle of a small rolling suitcase, he flashed his famous double-dimpled smile. "You travel lighter than your sister," he said before he took everything out to his car.

Harper was grateful Natthaniel Adams was in her

life. He was an honorable and dependable man just like her father. Natthaniel provided her comfort but she was sad for him because he was hopelessly in love with Sydney.

...continued in Towers Part Two - Stronger than Steel

Towers
The Ellison Legacy Part Two

Stronger than Steel
(Excerpt)

Loyalty
(Rubin)

Rubin never trusted the pigs. He wasn't saying shit to no cop, even if the cop was an attractive looking African-American woman. She spoke politely to him through his front gate, but after she showed her badge, Rubin told the Detective, "Talk to Sydney Ellison. She's in charge now. I ain't work construction in years. I ain't got nothing to say to you." Rubin was angry when the detective insisted on showing him a photo of damages to the building. The picture triggered flashbacks of the old accident he tried to forget. Rubin was not polite when he told Detective Stone if she didn't have no warrant to get off his porch.

Rubin was loyal to the Ellisons, they were his family. He still volunteered with Paul at the Mansa Center. Rubin was doing good, except sometimes when Paul's limp bothered his conscience. He looked forward to seeing his family at the welcome home dinner for Harper, but he was going to make a quick retreat after the dinner. Rubin wanted no parts of another Ellison tragedy and he did not want any more pigs visiting his house.

The Towers Series
The Ellison Legacy

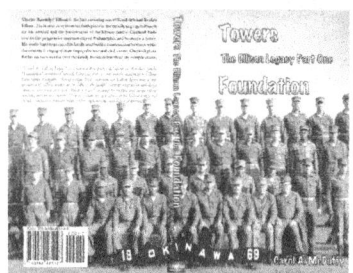

Part One - Foundation

Part Two - Stronger than Steel

Part Three - Built to Last